HER CAPTIVATED HERO

A BLACK DAWN NOVEL BOOK 6

CAITLYN O'LEARY

GW00643817

Dedicated to those who are serving and who have served.

1

A GUN IN A BAR?

Not on his fucking watch!

Gray Tyler lunged from his seat ready to kill. That was when he realized he was dealing with a dumbass of epic proportions.

Asshat fumbled for a gun stuffed in the back of his oil-stained, drooping jeans. Afraid he would get it tangled in his tighty-whities, Gray thought he might be permanently blinded by the sight of gunman's butt crack.

He ran across the crowded San Diego bar, hearing the crash of chairs that told him Dex and Griff, two of his SEAL team members, were at his back. Gray acted as blocker for his men as they plowed through the packed crowd toward the potential shooter.

Thank the good Lord, it was looking promising that the dumb oaf would plug himself in the ass before he pulled his pistol loose. But still, if Gray started trusting luck at his age, he wouldn't make it to thirty-seven. Gray shouldered a billionaire-wannabe out of his way, ensuring the petite blonde who'd been beside him stayed upright.

Fuck me running.

Droopy Drawers swung the gun upwards.

"Let go of my woman," the man slurred as he shot up into the ceiling. He stumbled as he continued. "Stella is mine. You stole her." The dumbass lowered his gun to point at some weasel hiding behind a woman in a gold miniskirt and pink thigh-high boots.

Really?

Gray thanked God that Griff and Dex's wives and the rest of the bachelorette party were busy whooping it up on the dance floor behind him, safely out of the line of fire.

Goddammit, would he have noticed this cretin sooner if his attention hadn't been so focused on the curvy bridesmaid who danced as though she were music in motion?

People started screaming as soon as the shot was fired. Shouts of "Gun," reverberated throughout the crowd. People were beginning to run and drop to the floor. Gray and his team needed to shut this shit down.

"Dex, left," Gray commanded. He didn't even need to see his man to know that he'd be on the left side of the shooter like white on rice.

"Griff, girlfriend."

With just those four words, his two subordinates understood that he planned to take out Droopy Drawers. Dex was going to be his back-up and Griff would ensure gold-miniskirt-girl stayed safe.

Since they were all special operations, the three of

them had concealed weapons permits. But pulling more guns in this situation was a bad idea, especially since this guy was drunker than a skunk.

"Leroy, she's mine now," Weasel-face yelled. "She's never coming back to you." The little man somehow showed enough courage to step out in front of Stella and plant his hands on his skinny hips.

Just how much stupid could be packed into three people?

Gray saw the shooter's forearm tense and flew those last seven yards across the wooden floor and slammed his wrist under the man's hand, causing the second shot to zing upward into the ceiling. He twisted the gun out of DD's hand, crashing his elbow into his neck. The shooter went down to the floor before he could say 'Boo'.

"Get off me, you asshole," a woman shrieked. Gray glanced up in time to see that Griff and Dex had the dishwater blonde and her weasel boytoy safely on the ground.

"Shit, man, you had him taken care of before I even knew what was going on," a big bouncer said as Gray was using the toe of his boot to turn DD over so that half his ass wasn't on display.

People started clapping, but it didn't drown out Stella. Gray shook his head in disgust when she pushed her way past the bouncer and dropped down on top of Droopy-Drawers.

"Leroy. My poor baby, are you all right? Did they hurt you?"

"Stella," he groaned.

She turned on Gray like a virago. "How dare you

3

attack him like that. What were you thinking? He wouldn't have shot me. He loves me."

She peppered kisses on her old boyfriend's face. Leroy groaned louder. Then he belched. Gray looked at Dex and they both took a step backward. Leroy let out a louder belch and moaned.

"You need an ambulance," Stella crooned as she wrapped her arms around his neck. Dex's eyes twinkled.

Gray backed up one more step, grabbing the bouncer's arm as he did so.

"Stella, I'm gonna—"

Vomit spewed from Leroy's mouth, into Stella's hair and continued on towards the bar room floor. Stella shrieked as she jumped up and back, skidding on her gold-sequined ass, but the damage was already done.

"I owe you twice," the bouncer grinned.

"How about you let us get back to our ladies over at the dance floor, and you deal with the deputies?" Gray suggested.

"Done." The bouncer agreed and then held out his hand. Gray shook it, then he handed over the pistol.

"Drinks for your party are on the house tonight," the younger man said.

"The whole bar will lose money," Griff joined the conversation. "We're babysitting a bachelorette party."

The big bouncer easily looked over the sea of people and saw the dance floor where Griff's wife and the other girls were. "Those ladies have been causing quite a stir tonight. Are they all taken, or are some of them single?"

4

Dex stiffened. "The strawberry blonde in green is definitely taken," he said darkly.

Was that Dex Evans? Gray would have bet a whole hell of a lot of money that his man Dex didn't have a jealous bone in his body.

Just goes to show, you don't know everything.

"How about the rest of you? Any claims?" The bouncer swung his head around.

"Willowy brunette is my wife, but she'll let you know fast enough," Griff laughed. "Just respect the rings man, and you'll be fine."

The young man nodded.

Gray looked over the man in the black T-shirt – he was at least ten years his junior and was in as good as shape as any SEAL. It rubbed him the wrong way that he might end up talking to the dancer that Gray had been watching.

"Ah shit," Griff groaned. "What now?"

Gray turned, his eyes narrowing.

"Kenna!" Dex tried to shout above the music, but the band was playing so loud, there was no chance that he could be heard. A tall, thin executive-type was standing over Dex's wife, his attention squarely centered on the alluring dancer behind her. Kenna had positioned herself in front of suit-guy, obviously trying to protect the dark-haired beauty. Gray groaned as he saw Dex's wife slap her hands on his chest. Thank God the idiot didn't touch Kenna, because there would have been hell to pay.

This time Dex led the charge, but before he got there to protect his woman, the pocket-sized Venus had wormed her way between Kenna and the executive.

The next thing Gray knew, the man was falling to the floor.

What the hell?

The eleven ladies who had been partying it up for the bachelorette party all let out a collective *whoop* of congratulations. Dex, Gray, and Griff arrived in time to see the guy up on his elbows, shaking his head.

By the time he got to the scene, he'd figured out what happened. He stopped dead in front of the beautiful woman he'd had his eyes on for most of the night. Gray held out his hand. "Give me the stun gun."

Almond-shaped golden eyes looked up at him innocently. "What are you talking about?" she murmured. Gray had been expecting an accent to go along with her exotic beauty, but she sounded born and bred American.

"Honey, the guy on the floor is still vibrating, you used some kind of stunner on him, and I'm going to hand it over to the bouncer. He's going to want to confiscate it for the rest of the time you're here."

"My name is Riya Patel," she corrected him. "But for the first time ever, I like the nickname Honey," her mouth twitched in a smile. Did he smell peaches or raspberries?

Damn, she made him feel like it was just the two of them, yet they were surrounded by at least a hundred people.

"Stun-gun," he quietly commanded.

Riya grinned at him mischievously. "You're not easily deterred, huh?" She held out the weapon instead of putting it back into her purse.

"Oh I think you might be able to dance around me,"

Gray smiled slowly, happy he was finally making contact with the woman who had been driving him insane all night long.

He heard Dex cough loudly behind him. If he wasn't mistaken, he was covering up a laugh.

"Lieutenant, here comes the bouncer," Dex warned.

Gray took the weapon, putting it under his jacket, and turned to see a different bouncer headed their way. Griff was helping the shaky executive to his feet.

"What seems to be the problem?" the bouncer asked roughly.

Ten women started to talk at once, but Riya stayed silent. She just moved closer to Gray and that was alright by him. The bouncer turned to the pin-striped-suit guy.

"I saw you go down. What happened?" he demanded.

"Nothing," the man answered shakily. "It was all a misunderstanding." He slid his way past the crowd of women and disappeared. Riya swayed in front of Gray and tried to whisk the gun out of his hand. He slid it into the back of his jeans, and grabbed her wrist instead. She looked up at him and rolled her eyes.

"Ladies, we don't need any problems here. You got me?" the bouncer glowered. Gray stifled a grin as he saw the younger bouncer from before come up behind the man giving the lecture.

"Harry, these guys just took down the shooter over near the Swing Bar," he said as he put his big hand on his co-worker's shoulder. "Phil said to set them all up with free drinks for the rest of the night. That includes their pretty lady friends."

Harry looked disgruntled. "There was a problem over here, Tony. One of these *ladies* took down a man, and I think she used some kind of stun-gun to do it." He pointed at Riya.

"Is the guy dead? Is he injured? Is he pressing charges? Where is he?" Tony smiled and winked at Riya as he shot out the questions. Gray put his hand around her tiny waist. Tony smiled even broader, as he watched Gray's less than subtle claim.

"He left," Harry admitted.

"Then we're done." Tony surveyed the women, and saw Griff with Miranda, Dex with Kenna and Gray's hand on Riya's waist. Tony then offered his arms to a blonde and to Susan, the bride-to-be. "Let me escort you ladies back to your table. Then I'll get Trixie to set you up with a round of drinks."

"So are you going to finally come and sit with us, instead of just watching from the back?" Riya asked as she peered up at Gray from beneath her bangs.

"I'm not sure Miranda and Kenna want their men honing in on their fun," Gray said.

Riya's eyes cut over to where Griff and Dex were settling in next to their wives, then looked pointedly back at Gray and grinned.

Dimples, she has dimples.

"Oh, I don't know," she teased.

He glanced back at the table. Yep, they were being welcomed, especially Griffin. Then Gray realized it probably wasn't that often that the young parents had a night out. His eyes narrowed when he saw that Kenna was drinking a glass of water, instead of the margaritas that the rest of the ladies were favoring. He looked over

8

at Dex and saw an even more proprietary gleam in his eye than when he had called off the bouncer.

Well hell. If he had to guess, Kenna was pregnant. It must be pretty recent news if Dex hadn't told him. *Good for them.*

"Okay, your point is taken," he admitted ruefully to Riya.

She grabbed his hand. Her grip was firm, despite the fact that his hand dwarfed hers.

"Come on." She tugged. She didn't pull him to the table. Instead, she tugged him toward the dance floor. Gray realized they were playing a sexy ballad.

"Are you sure?" he asked.

"You move like a jungle cat." Her smiled sparkled. "I would love to see what you're like on the dance floor."

Jungle cat? Who says that kind of thing?

"You're just making a play to get your gun back, aren't you?" he questioned.

"You'll just have to dance with me, and find out."

Her golden eyes flashed up at him. They were framed with the longest black lashes he'd ever seen, and Gray would bet his next paycheck they weren't false. The woman packed a punch in her low-ride jeans and T-shirt that didn't quite meet the top. It left a tantalizing swath of warm, honey-colored skin showing. No wonder the guy in the suit had been so enthralled. Hell, half the men in the place had their eyes on her.

"So tell me Riya, how do you know the bride?"

"Susan and Miranda work at TAID. Miranda's the project manager on the job I'm liaising with from UCSD. It's all really boring, but Susan and Miranda have made it fun."

Gray's radar went up. TAID worked on a lot of military applications. Griff was tightlipped about Miranda's job, but Gray had a good idea that she worked on some high-level shit, considering the fact she had been known to brief the Pentagon.

But Miranda had to be eight years older than Riya – this girl must be a grad student at the University of California San Diego. She tugged on his hand again, and he allowed her to pull him into the middle of the crowd of people. It wasn't a hardship.

When Riya reached up to twine her arms around his neck, he had to bend. She was a tiny little thing, but she was lush in all the right places. Gray kept his hands high on her upper back, now *that* was a hardship.

"Really?" She gave him a wicked grin, then reached back and placed one of his hands down onto the small of her back, where shirt didn't meet denim.

"What if I didn't want my hand there?" Gray asked as he moved them around the dance floor.

"You did," she said blithely.

He raised one blonde eyebrow.

"Didn't you?" Riya bit her lip.

It was the first time she showed the slightest bit of hesitation. He could play it two ways. In the end, he chose honesty.

"You read me right, Honey," he said. Then he bent down and whispered in her ear. "I'm just not sure I'm ready for this."

2

HAD HE REALLY JUST SAID THAT? GOD, SHE HOPED SO. Two peach Bellini's and she'd lost her damned mind.

Her sister Anika had given her that stun gun when she'd first started going to the university, and never in her wildest dreams had she thought she would use it. But she sure as hell wasn't going to allow some strange man push around Miranda's friend, he could have really hurt her. For the slightest second she'd been scared, then instinct had taken over and she'd had the weapon in her hand and the man was on the floor.

Okay, so she hadn't defended Kenna because of the alcohol, she would have done it no matter what. But taking off her jacket, when she knew that her shirt was riding up and showing her belly button? Well, that was definitely the fault of the second peach Bellini. She'd thought her shirt was okay when she left the house, but as soon as she started to move at the club she'd realized it wasn't staying in place so she was stuck with her jacket, but that thought flew out the window when she saw Gray.

So here she was in his arms, behaving like another woman, and loving every minute of it.

Thank God he was so strong, because he held her up when her legs turned to jelly. Not jelly, melted caramel. She clutched Gray's neck and inhaled his scent as she found herself pressed against his chest.

She shook her head just a little, trying to clear it.

"Does that mean you want to stop dancing?" he asked as they swayed together.

"Huh?" Her eyes shot up at him for just a quick moment, then she looked back down at the floor. "Oh, no, I love dancing, at least with you. I don't always like dancing, but with you, it's great. Just not always."

"Honey, just how much have you had to drink?"

"Two peach Bellinis," she admitted.

"I thought I smelled peaches and raspberries."

"The raspberries are from my shampoo." She shifted so that she could get a better grip on him. He looked down at her with crystal clear blue eyes.

"How often do you drink?"

"I don't know, once a quarter, maybe. I'm just feeling a little floaty. I couldn't have stunned idiot-boy if I was drunk, that took a little bit of focus and eye-hand coordination. But my inhibitions are lowered enough to appreciate how you look in your jeans and ask you to dance."

Riya slammed her face into his chest. Was it possible to smother herself in his shirt? She'd never heard of death by cotton, but she'd been the first in her class, why couldn't she be the first one in the world to kill herself this way?

She heard a low hum of laughter at the same time that she felt it against her cheek.

"So you like how I look in my jeans, huh?"

"A gentleman would have pretended he didn't hear that."

Gray moved her around the dance floor and then whispered in her ear. "You're right, a gentleman would not remind you of what you said." Gray slowed them down and once again they were swaying in place. Riya felt his thumb move. Just a little, then a little more. Then he began to draw intimate circles on the small of her back. It took everything in her not to shudder. Riya looked up and saw Gray watching her. The man knew the havoc he was wreaking.

"Can I tell you how much I like your shampoo? I think raspberries are the perfect metaphor for you, tart and sweet."

Gray Tyler spoke directly to her feminine core. Riya had seen him sitting off with Kenna and Miranda's husbands and there he'd seemed safe enough, but boy had she'd figured that wrong. Dex and Griff were cuddly teddy bears compared to Gray.

How long was this dance going to last?

Forever if she had anything to say about it. Somewhere in her hormone saturated brain she thought she heard the singer say something about a dress hitting the floor and the world going black. Riya felt her nipples tighten. Was it the song? Or was she picturing herself wearing a dress that Gray would peel off her body?

Gray applied the smallest bit of pressure and she swayed closer against his rock hard frame.

Am I out of my mind?

Why had Gray stopped moving? Darn it all, she'd liked the way their bodies had swayed and flowed together. Why were they standing still?

"The band's taking a break, Riya," Gray whispered softly.

That was when she realized everyone was leaving the dance floor. The music had stopped. She blushed. How had she missed it?

"I better get back to the girls." She pulled her hands away from his neck, but he didn't let her go.

"How are you getting home tonight?"

"Patty and I are sharing an Uber, why?"

"Then I was thinking I could spirit you away from the crowd and arrange for another Peach Bellini for you. I'd offer to pay, but they're on the house."

Riya giggled before she could stop herself and Gray raised an eyebrow in question.

"What?"

She bit her lip. "It's nothing. Why don't you tell me why the drinks are on the house."

"Why don't you tell me why you're giggling."

"Miranda and Kenna were right. You are a mother hen. She said that you outdid their husbands in spades."

He finally released her from his embrace, but kept his hand on her lower back as he began to escort her off the dance floor.

"Interesting. I'm going to have to disagree, though.

If anyone's ass is warm enough to hatch an egg, it would be Dex Evans."

Gray stopped as Riya stood in place, trying to stop her laughter. "Can I tell Kenna you said that?" she finally asked.

"I would be heartbroken if you didn't."

Riya smiled up at him as he continued to move them toward another part of the cavernous bar. "Now tell me why the drinks are on the house."

"There was a bit of an altercation over at the Swing Bar. The guys and I took care of it, so the bouncers decided to set you up."

"What happened?" Riya persisted. "What kind of altercation?"

It was obvious he didn't want to tell the full story. As a matter of fact, he looked a little bit uncomfortable. Riya liked it, because God knows, she'd been feeling off kilter since he'd started tracing circles on her back.

"Just some drunken joker who needed to prove his love...with a gun."

Riya stumbled, but Gray was there to keep her upright.

"A gun? Are you serious?"

"I wish I weren't."

Riya rapidly flipped through everything she had seen and heard during the last two hours while at San Diego's popular new dancehall. It was a huge complex, with three different bar areas and two separate dance floors. She'd heard yelling from the opposite side of the building, and what she'd thought had been the crack of chairs being broken. At that same time, the three military men weren't at their table.

"Let me get this straight. Are you saying those were gunshots that I heard, and not something else like I originally thought?"

Gray gave a slow nod.

The alcohol began to lift. "Interesting," she said slowly. "I heard some yelling as well, but no sirens. Is it safe to assume that you and your men were able to disarm this man who was trying to 'prove his love'?"

Gray's lips twitched.

"How do you know they are my men? Did Miranda tell you that they work for me?"

"She didn't say your rank, but I know that Griff is a POFC in a small SEAL team. They'd been talking about you earlier and said that you were the leader. That would make you the lieutenant, ergo, you."

"Ergo?" Gray's lip twitched.

"I know, I know," Riya waved her hand. "I always get teased for using that word. But I like using the right words when they fit the situation."

"Well, Ms. Patel, you have surmised correctly. I am Lieutenant Tyler. What else have you accurately deduced?"

"I like that word too," Riya grinned. She looked down as he clasped her hand. So cool, they were holding hands. There was so much to like. "Deduced, it just sounds good coming off your lips."

"I kind of like the word lips," Gray said as he continued to walk with her.

"Shhh, I'm deducing. Kind of like Sherlock Holmes." But now she was looking at his lips. *Come on Riya, play detective.* He raised his eyebrow for her to continue.

"Now this next part is conjecture, mind you."

He nodded.

"You, Dex and Griff were gone when I heard loud sounds that must have been the gunshots from the drunken joker. I am assuming you took him out in such a way that the police were only required to scoop him up and take him away. That must have been the reason why I didn't hear any sirens. If I had to take another guess, you're less than pleased that any shots were fired at all."

Gray had been slowing down with every word she uttered until they finally came to a complete stop.

"Am I right?"

Riya realized he was looking at her with an expression that she couldn't read, hardly a new sensation for her. Damn it, had she blown it? Was he thinking she was a freak because she could figure it out? She should know better than to act like some kind of know-it-all.

When will I learn?

Gray nodded solemnly. "You were right on the money, perfect marks. Something tells me you're used to getting perfect marks."

"Great, I got perfect marks," she sighed.

Yep, she should have kept her mouth shut. She'd ruined it again. But seriously, did she have to screw things up just minutes after he'd whispered sweet nothings in her ear? Her eyes felt gritty and she blinked fast. He'd even used the word *deduced*.

Riya looked over at her table. She could see the girls watching them with curiosity. He followed her glance.

Gray pulled his hand from hers and slid it to her

waist as he subtly turned her away from the bachelorette table. Riya looked up into his face but he was intent on guiding them through the crowd so that she wasn't jostled. Riya marveled that Gray managed to find the one open tall table against a wall next to the pool tables, in a corner that was relatively quiet.

"This okay?" he asked with a smile.

"Yes," Riya answered with wonder. "I thought you were going to head for the hills," she admitted softly. He was smiling, was that a good sign?

His blue eyes held hers, the eye contact making her feel uncomfortable. "Does that happen a lot?"

"Yes." She felt a sting and realized she was biting her lip. She sighed and decided to come clean. "But this time it would have mattered."

A red-headed waitress with a competent air appeared and Gray handed her the empty glasses that had cluttered the table.

"What would you like?" she asked Riya with a wide smile.

"Sparkling water with lime, if it isn't too much of a problem," Riya requested.

"Easy enough, Sweetie." She didn't write it down. Riya guessed that she'd been waitressing most of her life, and she looked like she enjoyed it. How great was that?

"And you, Tough Guy? You get to choose from the top of the shelf. Loved your take down. I'm betting military, not cop. Am I right?"

Riya watched as Gray gave her an easy grin. "Why are you betting on military?"

"My husband's a cop. He would have stuck around

to talk to the police. You and your buddies left it to our crew."

"Navy," Gray confirmed. "I'll take a sparkling water too, but just to keep you guessing, how about lemon? What's your name?"

"Rosie."

"I'm Gray, this is Riya," he smiled as he introduced them.

"Nice to meet you. I think I can keep your drinks straight," she winked and sidled through the crowd to the next table.

Riya settled on the edge of the tall seat, resting her forearms on the table, and played with the coaster. Gray covered her hands and that was when she noticed she'd started to tear the thing into confetti.

"I thought we established I wasn't running for the hills? As a matter of fact I culled you from the herd so we could get to know one another better."

Her lips twitched. "Interesting phrase. Do many of the women you meet like being compared to cows?"

Gray laughed. He had a great laugh.

"I've got to admit, that wasn't my smoothest line. So, are you part of the wedding party?"

"Bridesmaid number forty-seven."

Gray looked over her shoulder as Rosie came back to the table.

"Here's your water," Rosie said with a flourish as she set down two wine glasses. "Do you want me to pour?" She set the green bottle of Italian sparkling spring water along with a bowl of lemon and limes.

"I think I'll do the honors," Gray answered.

"Okay, I'll be back to check on you in a few."

"We're definitely getting the V.I.P. treatment." Riya noted. "Just how bad was the 'little altercation'?" she asked, using air quotes.

"On a scale of one to ten, it didn't even make it onto the scale," Gray said seriously as he filled her glass.

She considered what he said, and immediately decided she needed to read up on Navy SEAL operations.

"What would make it on the scale?" she asked.

"Bridesmaid forty-seven? Sounds like it's going to be a big wedding."

"Got it, no more talking about work," Riya laughed.

"We could talk about yours. What does liaising with TAID entail? What exactly do you do?"

Damn, couldn't this wait until the second date?

"Riya?" Gray prompted with a lazy smile.

She sighed.

"I'm a scientist. One of my doctorates is in Molecular Virology, and I spend a lot of time in the lab trying to get a handle on arenavirus molecular and cell biology. Maybe we can go back to me describing my bridesmaid dress? Wouldn't that be more interesting?"

"Mmmm, my choice is lilac colored chiffon or what I can remember from the not so fun part of high school biology? I think I need to call Rosie back and ask for a beer. Then again, I'm not sure I want my brain too foggy with a woman with two doctorates. Please tell me it's only two," Gray pleaded with a sinful smile. He then gently pulled yet another coaster out of her hands.

She started to relax. "It's only two," she assured him.

"Good. I think if you'd said three I would have started having an inferiority complex."

"Do you need anything else?" Rosie asked them as she passed by their table.

"I'm good, how about you Riya?"

"I think I'm good, too."

"You are definitely a couple of steps up from good." Gray enjoyed watching a soft blush wash over her face. "So, I'm guessing you can't really talk about what you're working on right now since it's with Miranda, right?"

"Right."

"Do you like working with her?"

Riya's eyes lit up. "Hell yeah. She's kick-ass."

"Have you seen her in action? From what Griff tells me, on rare occasions she has been known to eviscerate someone who's tried to undermine a project she's in charge of."

"Susan calls it the Porter Surgical Strike."

"I like it," Gray said admiringly.

"I've only seen her do it once. The woman deserved it. She'd been undermining one of the men on our project for months, but he'd never said anything. We were in a staff meeting when it became obvious what she was doing. In three sentences Miranda handed this woman her ass. Miranda was professionally contemptuous, and you could see this woman shrink in her seat. She stuttered out an apology to Bill. It was beautiful."

"Did this woman ever try to undermine *you*?" Gray asked.

"She tried. But I'm not as easy of a target as I look.

More than that, she couldn't really understand what I was working on, so there was no way she could try to take credit for what I was doing."

"So what's your second doctorate in?"

"Microbiology."

"Were you always a science geek?" Gray immediately regretted his teasing question when he saw Riya pick up another random coaster off the table. He knew she was going to start ripping it to pieces.

"Hey, Steven Hawking is one of my idols." He smiled as he pulled one of her hands across the table and forced her to drop the coaster. Gray rubbed his thumb along the line between her heart and life lines. "The way your head line curves, you're a creative thinker who imagines many approaches and outcomes to a situation. Is that you, Riya?"

She tried to pull her hand away, but he continued his gentle hold. "I wouldn't have thought a military man would read palms. How do you know the characteristics of the head line?" He watched her hunch her shoulders.

He continued to caress her palm. "I didn't mean to upset you."

"I'm not upset," she protested. "Why do you like Steven Hawking?" Riya questioned.

"Are you changing the subject?"

She hunched her shoulders further and shook her head, her long black hair flew around her, shielding her face.

"I guess."

"I read *A Brief History of Time*. Some of it made sense, some of it didn't but most of it made me think of things in a much broader context. Then I watched the movie *The Theory of Everything* and realized how that disease was ravaging his body..." Gray shook his head. "He was an amazing man."

Riya smiled. "You're right. I met Dr. Hawking once. His spirit is overwhelming."

"Now will you tell me what I did to upset you?"

She gave him a wry smile. "I have issues," she admitted. "I guess questions sometimes feel intrusive. It reminds me of when I was little and all the tests they used to administer."

"What tests?" he asked gently.

"I.Q. tests," she sighed.

Again she tugged at her hand. This time he released it and watched her cup her water glass with both hands that trembled ever so slightly.

"Sounds a little like Sniper training. You're tested all the damned time. I've never been through such intense training and testing in my life."

He watched as she relaxed enough to pick up her glass and take a sip of water. "Really?"

"Oh yeah. Less than half of us would graduate, and trust me it was a rigorous selection process to get in."

She smiled slowly. It was a punch in the gut. "But you graduated."

Gray nodded.

"So you're a sniper and a lieutenant?"

"Yep. Are you a genius?"

She grinned. "Because I figured out you were a sniper? Yep."

"So you're a smartass and a genius. My favorite combination. Tell me about your testing." Gray encouraged as he refilled her glass. "Why was it so bad?"

"My parents were first generation Americans. They came from Bangladesh and didn't understand the Californian school system, and were confused by some of the things the teachers were telling them. In their defense, I think they were getting conflicting information. This started when I was in kindergarten. It took a while before they were able to navigate the school system and get me properly tested."

"How did they figure it out in the end?"

"Because nobody could agree on anything, they left me in normal classes, so by second grade I began acting out and I was flagged as having behavioral problems."

"That must have been tough," he commiserated.

Her dark eyes sparkled. "Actually there were times I made the most of it. If I was expected to act out, I really acted out."

"How old were you?"

"I was seven," she said.

"So how did seven-year-old Riya act out?"

He couldn't wait to hear this.

"We used nothing but pencils to turn in our work, right?"

Gray nodded.

"One day I managed to hide in the coat closet while everyone else went to recess. I erased everyone's name off the papers they'd handed into the teacher."

Gray laughed. He loved it.

"Did you have your hair in a long dark braid?"

Riya's eyes got wide. "How'd you know?"

"I could just picture it. You were probably the

picture of innocence, nothing but beautiful black hair and big black eyes. Did they suspect you?"

"Not Mrs. Ayers, but the counselor did. But he couldn't prove it." She squeezed another slice of lime into her water. "Luckily, my second grade teacher graduated from UCLA, so she was affiliated with the California University systems. She ended up getting me correctly tested at UC San Diego. She worked with my parents and walked them through the system."

"Was it overwhelming?"

"My parents got really excited when they found out I could be part of a research study, so yeah, it was a lot of testing. I absolutely despised the exams, but once I got into the meat of the classes, I thrived. Not every child did."

Riya's eyes got wide with surprise. "I've never shared all of this with anyone outside of work. What kind of palm reading magic did you do?"

"If I told you, then it wouldn't be magic."

Riya gave him a considering look. "I'm thinking the real magic is that you're nice."

Hell, the last time he'd been called that had probably been as a child. At eighteen he'd entered the Naval Academy and left there a man and an officer. Later he became a SEAL.

Nice? That hardly entered into it.

Good. He strove to be a good man. Hell, not even Felicia, who he'd lived with for two years had called him nice. When they'd split, and they'd split on fucking great terms, she hadn't called him nice. Nope, she'd called him impeccably fair.

"You still with me?" Riya asked.

"I'm just trying to get over the fact you called me nice," he admitted. "I'm trying to determine if I like it or not."

"I meant it in a good way, if it matters."

She was adorable. Then she bit her lip. Next thing she'd be reaching for a coaster. "I know you meant it in a *nice* way." Gray gave her his best smile.

"Whoa, your smile sure does pack a punch." She put her elbow on the table and rested her chin on her hand. "If you don't like being called a nice guy, how *should* I describe you?"

"Let's not pigeonhole one another. I say we take some time to get to know each other."

"How much time?"

It was fun seeing her back to flirting. "Well we're almost done with this bottle of water, want to go for another?" Gray asked.

She sat up straight and shook her head. "I'll end up floating out of here if I have any more. What else do you have?"

Oh yeah, the sparkle in those black eyes had him thinking all kinds of naughty things. "I can think of something. How about if we discuss my ideas as I get you back to your friends?"

"Sure, we can head back," she said as she quickly hid her disappointment behind a bright smile. It reassured him that his next step was the right one.

Riya slid off the high stool. "I've probably been gone long enough. You want to lead the way?" she asked. She waved her arm to indicate he step ahead of her.

"I was hoping you'd let me lead." Gray trailed his fingers from the inside of her elbow down to the tips of her fingers, watching her shudder. "Let's not hurry," he said as he sidestepped her outstretched hand and pushed into her personal space. He bent toward her so they were almost nose to nose. She looked down at the floor. Her sudden shyness intrigued him.

"Lead where?"

"First there was dancing, then there was conversation, I have an idea for the next step in our getting to know one another sequence."

Her eyes widened beneath her thick lashes. "I do a lot of sequencing in my job. In fact, I really enjoy it. Will this be as fun as dealing with next-generation sequencers?"

Gray barked out a laugh. "I'll give it my best shot."

He traced his knuckles from the top of her cheek, down the silky trail to her jaw, then he moved his thumb so that it tested the tantalizing plump softness of her lower lip.

Riya looked up, watched him intently. Then he moved his palm so he could cup her jaw. She was so delicate. His little finger caressed the shell of her ear and she let out the smallest cry of need as her eyelids fluttered shut. Riya swayed against him and he felt the stiff rasp of her nipples between their clothes.

God, she was killing him, and he hadn't even tasted her.

"Gray?" She whispered his name and it was flavored with lime and another essence that he couldn't define, but he needed to explore.

"I'm here," he assured her. Then he touched his lips to hers.

For some reason he couldn't fathom, Riya was

tentative. All of the sass and confidence that she'd exhibited on the dance floor had deserted her, but Riya's innate sultry heat shone through. Her arms crept up his chest and then higher. Gray shuddered as her warm hands crafted magic against his skin. He felt like he had slipped into a dark night where only the two of them existed.

His eyes opened as she whimpered.

He curled his arms around her and walked her backwards so that she was ensconced in a dark corner, hiding her behind his big body.

She'd caught fire. He traced his tongue along the seam of Riya's plush lips, and she welcomed him inside. Heat exploded and he tasted the flavor of her passion.

Arousal hit Gray low and hard. It took everything he had not to lift her up and wind her legs around his hips. Where was his calm? Where was his composure?

Shot to shit, that's where.

He squeezed his eyes shut, fighting for a semblance of control. When his head stopped spinning, Gray stroked a soothing hand down the side of Riya's trembling body. It took long moments for her to come back to herself. Thank the good Lord he wasn't the only one in a state of extreme need.

"Uhmm," she murmured as she rested her head against his chest. "Sequence?" she finally croaked out.

Gray smoothed his hand down her long, silky black hair. "That got out of hand. I'm sorry."

Her head jerked up, her eyes wounded. "You are? You're sorry?" She gave him a forlorn look.

"I'm not sorry for kissing you," he said. "I'm sorry

that something so passionate, so intimate, wasn't done in a private place."

"Oh." Her smile was slow to come, but when it did, it dazzled. "We should arrange some private time."

His mind boggled at the thought as his hands moved up to rest on her shoulders. "Honey, I think we need to take things a little slower than that. Do you have a date to Susan and Mike's wedding?"

She shook her head.

"Would you like to be mine?"

She nodded her head.

"Good answer."

"Do I get another kiss?" she asked hopefully.

He touched the end of her nose. "Not here. Not now."

"I knew you were going to say that," she pouted.

"That's because you're a genius. Now why don't you give me your address."

Riya fumbled with her cross-body purse. He stayed her hand. "Just tell me. I'll remember."

She rattled off an address in a trendy neighborhood west of San Diego.

"Got it. Now let me take you back to the ladies before they send out a search party."

"Oh my God, you're totally right."

3

Einstein jumped down off the bathroom counter when the doorbell rang.

"Bad Kitty!"

Einstein meowed back at her with haughty disdain. He hated being called 'Kitty'. He stalked toward the bathroom door and Riya looked at the makeup, brushes and spilled lotion on the floor.

"I should have capped that properly," she said.

She heard another meow. The damned cat was agreeing with her. She turned and glared at him, and then he turned around and walked out of the bathroom. She grabbed some tissue and wiped up the mess and the doorbell rang again.

What an auspicious start to the day. Riya tore down the stairs with Einstein trailing behind her.

When she got to the door, she took a deep breath and smoothed down the silk of her blue dress that fell to just above her knee. Opening the door, she was met with miles and miles of chest covered by a blue pinstripe suit and silver tie. Her knees weakened. Riya had to look at least a foot into the air to briefly meet Gray's clear blue eyes. They matched her dress. Thank God she wasn't wearing her shoes, or she really would topple over.

The only thing that kept his smile from looking like a toothpaste ad was that he had a little scar that bisected his upper lip. She wanted to lick it. Oh yeah, she had it bad.

Heat suffused her body as the memory of that amazing kiss overloaded her senses.

"If you keep looking at me like that, we're not going to the wedding." His voice rumbled like thunder.

Arggh. If she wasn't careful she'd get drool on her dress. Everything she'd practiced saying to him totally flew out of her mind. She needed to get a handle on this, like yesterday. Still, he was good to look at.

"No can do, sailor. I'm a bridesmaid, I have commitments. Why don't you come on in and sit down. I still have to get their package wrapped."

Riya turned and waved him in and shut the door. When she turned back she saw him standing in the middle of her living room with his left eyebrow reaching for his hairline.

"Having trouble making up your mind?" he asked.

She let out a long sigh. "Laugh. Just get it over with. It's not like I haven't heard it before."

"Do you own a craft shop? Does someone in your family own stock in Hallmark?" Gray asked as he bent down and picked up two rolls of wrapping paper and compared them.

"I want to make sure that it's pretty and conveys the right message," Riya said as she snatched the rolls from his hand. Gray simply bent down and picked up two more rolls.

"Honey, I've seen people with a variety of Christmas wrap, but how many different patterns of wedding wrap do you have here?"

Riya looked at her six large Tupperware bins, five that contained wrap and one that contained ribbon and bows. "Can I say that I don't know?"

Gray tapped one of the bins with the toe of his high polished shoe. "You'd be lying. I bet you know the entire inventory of your house. How many rolls?"

"Fifteen wedding, seven baby shower, five Hanukkah, thirty-seven Christmas, two Easter, five Valentines, twenty-seven birthday rolls of wrapping paper and one St. Patrick's day," she reluctantly admitted.

Gray took a moment, then he gave her a sympathetic smile. "It must kill you to be one roll shy of one hundred."

Dammit, he was right. It *was* killing her. She was down a roll since Ethan's birthday. Gray must have seen he'd been on target because he laughed.

"How can I help?" he asked.

"I just have to get the present wrapped and find my shoes, then we're good to go."

"I don't believe that you can't find your shoes."

Neither did she. They were supposed to be right by the couch. She had precisely placed them perpendicular to the sofa right before she brought out the Tupperware containers.

"And if I offered to wrap the present while you found your shoes?" Gray asked. His eyes were sparkling. Again, he knew the answer to his question.

"Ahhhh," she tried to come up with an answer.

"How about if I pick out a wrapping paper or a ribbon?"

"You're totally getting a kick out of my obsessive compulsive nature, aren't you?"

Gray put the rolls of paper back down into the plastic bin and stepped toward her. "I just get a kick out of you. Full stop. The fact that you can laugh at yourself, is just the cherry on top of the sundae."

Riya tilted her chin up so she could look at him. "Don't you mean the sprinkle of nuts on the sundae?"

Gray chuckled. "See what I mean?"

That laugh. Those eyes.

Get a grip, girl.

She grabbed at his wrist so she could see his watch.

"The wedding starts in two hours and ten minutes," he said. "You have fifteen minutes to get your sexy tush in gear and out the door. That way we will be at the church exactly one hour before the ceremony is due to start. According to Griff that's when the bridesmaids are due to arrive."

"I can do this. Here's the deal. I just need to prioritize and delegate."

"Oh, I get to do something? I'm honored."

"You're a SEAL so you get to go on a rescue mission. Find my shoes. Last time I saw them they were exactly by the couch. I was walking around down here making sure I got used to them, since I'd never worn them before. After I made sure I wouldn't slip, I put them there." She pointed to where she had last seen them.

"Aye, aye." He tapped her on the nose and turned to gaze around the first floor of her townhome.

Riya bent down and pulled out the silver wrapping paper with rings and doves on it. She had some great sparkly silver ribbon to go with it, but didn't have time to mess with it, so it was time to use the big elegant bows that she'd been saving for a time crunch.

She ran to her kitchen, to the drawer that housed her scissors, and then skidded back into the living room in her stockings. Gray was standing there with her white patent leather pumps in his hands. "Are these what you were looking for?"

"Where'd you find those?"

"Your cat helped me find them. They were underneath the loveseat."

Riya crouched down and saw two shining blue eyes looking at her from beneath the sofa. "He didn't try to scratch you, did he?"

"Nope, we came to an understanding. What's his name?" Gray asked.

"Einstein. He's more temperamental than his namesake."

"Intelligent though. He saw me looking around and pushed one of the shoes out from under the sofa. It was the damndest thing."

"He was also the one who shoved them under there in the first place. He loves playing hide 'n seek." Riya knelt down and pulled the first box off of the coffee table. Gray peered over her shoulder and whispered.

"I didn't see those knives on the gift registry. They're high-end."

"Susan loves to cook. My mom swears by this brand. She's constantly saying that having the right tool for the job makes the meal."

"That's right for any mission." Gray picked up the second box and turned it over. "You also got grilling tools and utensils, another thing not on the wedding registry."

"I take it you shopped on the registry and had it sent to their house."

"I don't have ninety-nine rolls of wrapping paper to choose from." Gray turned over the corner of the paper she had chosen. "Are you sure this is the right one to use? It might be too much silver."

Riya blew her bangs out of her face and looked over her shoulder. "I got the impression you wanted to possibly see sunrise. Was I wrong about that?"

Gray held up his hands. "Note to self, no pithy comments on the lady's taste."

"Not if you want to live," she agreed.

"It's nice you got something for both of them. At least I'm assuming Mike grills."

"Does a bear poop in the woods?" Riya asked as she measured and cut the paper.

It's the prettiest paper, isn't it?

She folded the paper over and went to grab the tape. Gray had already torn pieces of tape and had them ready for her to grab. "You're prepared."

"Part of the job, ma'am."

She quickly had the knives and grill set wrapped with the bows on.

"How much more time?"

"You've got enough time to get your shoes on," Gray smiled.

"I've got to put the lids back on the paper before Einstein decides to play," Riya said as she bent over.

BEFORE HE COULD OFFER to do it, Riya was on all fours and fishing around under her couch and pulling out Tupperware lids. Gray took note of the intricate tattoo that was on display with her halter dress. It was a delicate lacy mandala between her shoulder blades, inked in black and orange.

Holy hell.

Now her dress was creeping up and her butt was wiggling. Had he died and gone to heaven?

Damn it.

He cleared his throat.

Riya pushed up on her knees, and pulled out a stack of lids.

"Give those to me, Honey. We're on a deadline, I'll put them on for you. You go sign the card."

She stood up and smoothed down her dress. When she was standing in front of him, he looked down at her as her head came up to the middle of his chest.

"I've been remiss," he said. She tilted her head and looked up at him. "I didn't tell you first thing that you look absolutely gorgeous."

Riya's face suffused with color as she looked away.

"Thanks," she mumbled. She bent her head and looked around the room. "There's the card." She hurried over to the dining room table and pulled a pen out of her purse. He saw her pause and then take her time to write something appropriate.

She grabbed her card, her purse and a shopping bag she'd had sitting by the card and came over to the couch. "Can you hand me my shoes?" she asked as she sat down.

Gray grabbed them and knelt down in front of her. "Let me help put these on."

"I can do it."

He traced his thumb over her cute toes, then slipped her peep-toe shoe on. He repeated the process with the second shoe, garnering another sigh from her. He wanted a kiss, but there wasn't a chance in hell he was going to risk it here in her home before they had to be somewhere. Especially not on their first date.

She got up from her seat and went over to the table and opened up the shopping bag.

"Gray, can you slip the packages in here?"

"Sure thing."

He picked up her white trench coat lying across the sofa and helped her put it on.

"Thank you, you're quite the gentleman."

"I was raised in Missouri. My two aunts would kill me if I failed to live up to the Southern gentleman standard."

She wrinkled her nose. "I didn't think Missouri was a Southern state."

"I grew up in Springfield. According to my great-grandfather who was still alive when I was eight, he said his father and uncles fought for the Confederacy.

My aunts only hold onto the Southern etiquette and hospitality something fierce."

He escorted her out of the condo. Outside, he snagged the umbrella he had left by the side of her entrance.

"You brought an umbrella?"

"There was a possibility of rain. Figured you would have a fancy hairdo, and you do," he smiled easily. "Give me your keys and I'll lock your door."

Riya handed over her keys, then frowned at him when he went to pocket her keys after he locked the door. "Give those back to me."

"No can do. I have to be able to unlock it when I bring you back."

"Uhm Gray, isn't that kind of control freaky?"

"Nope."

"I can't believe you said that with a straight face. That is so much being a control freak. Miranda warned me about that." His gaze slipped sideways and he watched as she thought over a new way to approach him. "Wouldn't it be more comfortable for me to have the keys in my purse instead of you having them in your pocket?" she reasoned.

"Nope."

He helped her into the passenger seat, then got into the driver's seat.

"Is it really important for you to be able to unlock the door for me when we get back?"

Gray liked the fact that she never sounded upset, just curious. It made him relax.

"Yes, it is."

She sat back in her seat. "Well, okay then."

Gray pulled out into the little side street and Riya concentrated on the bougainvillea lining the fences.

"So how well do you know Susan?" Gray asked.

"I've been working with her about a year. She's been a lifeline for me at the lab, and she's let me babysit for her. Plus she has a dog. And a cat. And a rabbit. I love it over at her house."

Riya clamped her hand over her mouth. Then immediately took it away to see if any of the lipstick came off. Good, it didn't. It was living up to the hype. But seriously, she needed to stop saying everything that came into her head.

"It sounds like you didn't come from a large family if you're so excited about babysitting a girl, a boy, a dog, a cat and a rabbit."

"How do you know Susan's kids are a girl and a boy?"

"I met them when they were little."

"You did?" She looked over at him curiously.

"It's a long story. So no brothers and sisters, or was it that you were just whisked away for schooling?"

"I was the youngest child of five girls. Amira, my sister closest to me in age is six years older than me. Then when I went to school I was always in grades with older kids, so I didn't get to interact with kids my own age. Plus, I was so busy studying I didn't have a chance to do anything like babysit when I was growing up, so spending time with Hope and Jeremy is a pleasure. What about you? Siblings?"

"I was raised by my two aunts, and spent a lot of

time over at the Conway's house. They had three kids and five foster kids, so they really didn't notice that one more was at their table most nights." Gray tilted his head. "There's the church."

Riya looked and saw the building through a faint haze of drizzling rain. The parking lot was full. Gray drove to the front entrance of the church and idled the car, then pressed a button on his steering wheel.

A man's voice came over the speaker, "Hello."

"Hey Griff, you got Miranda settled?" Gray asked.

"Affirmative."

"Can you come out front and escort Riya in, while I park?" Gray asked.

"I'll be there in a moment," Griff answered.

Gray disconnected.

"Isn't this taking the Southern gentlemen etiquette a little too far?" Riya asked.

"Not really," Gray said looking over at her. "Griff would have asked me to do the same thing for Miranda if the situation were reversed, and he was born and raised in Los Angeles. So this isn't a Southern gentleman thing, this is a Navy thing."

Suddenly her door opened, surprising her. Riya hadn't even noticed that Griff had come out of the church.

"Hi Riya," Griff grinned. He held out his hand for her. "You look gorgeous."

She looked over her shoulder at Gray in surprise. That's exactly what he had said. She wasn't used to all the praise.

I should get out of the lab more often.

Gray reached over and unhooked her seatbelt, then

he brushed the side of her cheek. "I'll be there in a minute, after I park the car." Then he looked over her shoulder. "Make sure she doesn't slip in those shoes. It's beginning to drizzle."

"Sure thing," Griff said.

She could practically smell the testosterone in the air.

"Uhm, gentlemen, I have made it almost twenty-six years without falling on my butt, thank you very much."

Griff took her hand and she stepped out of the vehicle. The pointed heel slipped out from beneath her, and if it hadn't been for Griff's quick reflexes she would be sitting in a puddle in the church parking lot.

Perfect, just perfect.

Her purse had fallen and everything was scattered to the four winds. She'd just bought that lipstick.

By the time she looked up from the security of Griff's arms, Gray's SUV was no longer idling. Instead it was in park, and Gray was pulling her out of his team member's arms.

"I've got you. Are you okay?" Gray demanded. She looked up into his face. His voice had come out all angry, but his eyes were the soft blue of concern and worry, not the mad blue. Which was it? Angry or concern? God, she hated not being able to read people.

Suck it up buttercup.

She gave a fake smile.

"How did you move that fast?" She looked over at his vehicle, then back at Griff who was crouched at her feet gathering up all of the things that had fallen out of her purse and putting them back in.

Really? A tampon? Kill me now. Where's a hole I can crawl into?

She looked up at Gray to see if he noticed, but he was staring down at her face. "You're looking flushed. Let's get you inside."

"Here you go," Griff handed her the purse.

"Here're my keys, can you park the SUV while I get Riya situated?" Gray asked.

"Sure thing," Griff smiled.

"I'm really capable of walking by myself." But as she looked at the wet steps leading up to the church, and considered her brand new high heels, having someone to hold onto sounded like a great idea. Darn it, she really needed to have gone for girly classes or shorter, thicker heels. But as soon as she'd seen these shoes at Nordstrom, it was a done deal. By golly, she'd intended to look tall and sleek walking down the aisle with the groomsman. What was his name again?

"Honey, you're daydreaming. Are you ready to go?"

She looked up and saw that she and Gray were standing under an umbrella. How had she not noticed that happening? She relaxed, this was definitely nice and concerned Gray.

"Let's get this show on the road." She nodded.

Gray put a bracing arm around her shoulder and the other under her elbow. Riya felt surrounded as they walked up the stairs. She took her time considering the sensation, and by the time they reached the top she decided it made her feel safe.

"That's quite the smile," Gray said as he closed the umbrella underneath the eves of the church.

"I've decided I like how your aunts raised you," she murmured.

His eyes brightened, and when they did little laugh lines fanned out from the corner of his eyes. "Let's get you in with the rest of the beautiful women, shall we?"

She shivered at the compliment. Oh yes, she definitely liked how he'd been raised.

AT THE RECEPTION, RIYA WAS PRACTICALLY BOUNCING UP and down in her chair. Her black eyes sparkled. Riya had teased Gray the entire short drive from the church to hotel where the reception was being held. Miranda and Griff's two-year-old daughter had seen him as they were leaving the church and had yelled out for her Uncle Gay-Gay. She wanted to be held and cuddled. Gray loved his honorary niece, but he was sincerely looking forward to the day that she would start calling him Uncle Gray.

"Did you see it all, Gray? You were seated near the back, and over to the right, so I didn't know if you could catch it all. I was dying. I laughed so hard, I was crying. I tried not to make any noise."

"Admit it Dr. Patel, you were crying, and it wasn't because you were laughing."

She bit her lip. "Okay, to begin with I was laughing, but then I was crying, crying. How could you not? It was so touching."

Gray had watched as every single bridesmaid had cried. He'd even choked up. "It was one for the record books, that's for sure."

"I adore Susan's kids."

Jeremy had been the ring bearer, and Hope had been the flower girl. When Susan had said, "I do," Hope had walked right over to her brother, grabbed his arm and dragged him up to the dais where the couple stood in front of the minister.

Mike and Susan, full of joy at the moment, had done nothing but smile at the two small children.

"I do, too, Mike," Hope had said in that high pitched voice of hers, still stuck between a baby and a little girl. "Are you my daddy now?" she'd asked.

Mike had swept the child up high into his arms, "I am definitely your Daddy if you want me to be."

Gray knew that Susan's first husband had died while serving overseas when Jeremy had been a toddler.

"Can I say 'I do,' too?" the six-year-old boy had asked.

Mike crouched down so he would be eye level with the child. "Absolutely, Champ."

"Can I call you Dad?" the young boy asked with a slow gap-tooth grin.

Mike cleared his throat. "I would be honored."

The ministered coughed. "Would this fine family like to turn around so we can finish the ceremony?" he'd asked kindly.

"Yay!" Hope cried. "We's getting married."

Gray shook his head, coming back to the present and looked around the ballroom. He spotted the little girl in question, then smiled back at Riya. "Yes, I saw the whole thing. It's going to be tough for any wedding to top that one."

"Look at Hope out on the dance floor. She is definitely in her element." Riya's smile was soft.

"Is she that much of a handful when you babysit her?"

"I usually have structured play time, so there isn't a lot of wiggle room for her to do too much outside of the parameters."

"Is that fun for her?"

Riya's eyes got even brighter. "Since I never babysat before, I was really worried about what to do. So I researched it. The kids seemed to like it, and I conferred with Susan afterwards and she said that they wanted me to come over and play again, even if I wasn't babysitting. So I'm thinking it was a success."

He was curious what the little scientist would have found to play with the young children. The fact that she'd researched it, slayed him. "What did you do?" he asked.

"Well, I wanted to do something that would both entertain them and teach them. I was always happiest when I was learning something as a kid."

"Is that true now?" Gray wasn't surprised, but he wanted to hear more about her childhood.

"Oh yeah, I love new experiences," she grinned. "For instance, this wedding has been fantastic. I've only ever been to one wedding before, and it was an Indian wedding. This was totally different."

He watched her eyes jump to the dance floor again, but before he could ask her to dance, she was talking.

"I bought Jeremy and Hope sketch pads and a bucket so that we could do a nature walk along the bike trail near Susan's house. I asked them to find different kinds of plants and flowers and put them into the bucket, and then sketch the different kinds of bugs, lizards and birds that they saw. I had planned to go back to the house so we could research everything they had found on the internet."

Gray smothered a grin as he asked, "How'd that work out?"

Riya frowned a little bit. "Actually things didn't go as planned."

"Really?" Again, he tried to keep a straight face.

"I had talked to Susan about my plan initially and she was enthusiastic about it, and said I should definitely try it."

"Hmmmm."

"So we got close to a little stream, and Jeremy heard frogs. That's when everything went to hell."

"He wanted to catch frogs," Gray guessed.

"I just thank God the stream was only five inches deep, but it was almost all mud."

"I told them that frogs are impossible to catch, and he told me that his mother let him catch them all the time."

"And you believed him?"

"How did you know he'd lied?" Her eyes were wide as she asked the question. He couldn't help it. He couldn't. He swept in for a swift kiss.

"I was a little boy once, I would have done anything to play in a creek, even lie. So what happened next?"

"Oh, Gray." She laughed and moaned at the same

time. "That wasn't a stream, it was a slow moving mud puddle. "Jeremy jumped in with both feet, and was covered from head to toe. He was in heaven. Then Hope was crouching down wanting to hunt for frogs."

"How muddy did you get?"

"By the time we got home, I had to strip all three of us down and throw everything into the wash machine. I had to steal some of Susan's clothes. Thank God her wash machine is close to the backdoor."

"Did you catch any frogs?"

"Not a one. Hope came the closest, that's why I had to shampoo her hair three times."

"I bet the kids had a ball."

Riya looked at Gray in amazement. "How did you know? I thought the day was an unmitigated disaster, and instead I'm now considered their favorite babysitter."

"What's on the agenda next time?"

"I want to teach them how to make homemade ice cream in a plastic bag. I just hope that we don't make a mess."

Gray couldn't stop his bark of laughter. "I don't know how you do that, but having a four- and six-year-old make ice cream in a plastic bag sounds like all kinds of a mess. Hell, having my SEAL team do it, sounds like a mess waiting to happen."

"Nuh-uh. I've read up on you guys. Only the best and the brightest make it in. You have to adapt on the fly. You're open to new situations, new stimuli, and like to compete. You succeed in what you set out to accomplish."

Gray tilted his head. "You read up on us?"

"I bought six books, I've only had time to read three. Then there were two studies. One was fascinating, it was the Personality Profile of SEALs."

Gray hadn't found and read that particular study until he was a Lieutenant.

"You're amazing."

"No I'm not, remember me? Research is my life."

She had a point. He needed to stay on top of his game with this woman. "So did you read anything that scared you off?"

"Everything I read made me happy for Miranda." Her mouth twitched and her eyes sparkled.

The little minx.

Nope, he wasn't going to ask. She finally started to laugh. "I kind of thought it was a good thing for me, too. That is if we go out on a second date."

"You can take that to the bank."

Gray stood up and held out his hand. Riya looked up at him confused.

"Can I have this dance?" he clarified.

She jumped up from her chair. "Absolutely."

Once more he was charmed by her delighted response.

"Ooops," she said. It was then he realized she was short again. Before she had a chance to crawl under the table and every man in the thirty yard radius had a chance to ogle her butt, he volunteered to fish out her shoes.

"You don't have to," Riya protested.

Gray crouched down and grabbed her shoes.

"Oh yes I do, trust me," he grinned ruefully, as he held up the first shoe.

"Aren't you going to hand them to me?"

"I'm going to help put them on." Gray realized he was developing a foot fetish.

She put her hands on his shoulders for balance, then arched her foot and he slid it on the first shoe. Gray couldn't resist smoothing his hand up her calf as he helped set her foot down onto the ground. Then he held up the next one.

"I think you're enjoying this," she said, clearly surprised.

"Ya think?"

She looked more closely at him.

"Yes, I do," she said with an impish smile.

He took his time putting on the second shoe, again stroking her tantalizing silk-clad leg. Then Gray rose from his crouch and took both of her small hands in his. "Dating a genius comes in handy. They understand what's going on."

He kept her close to his side as he maneuvered them through the tables and out to the wooden floor. It couldn't have worked out more perfectly if he'd orchestrated it himself, the DJ started to play an old standard from the forties.

"Who's this? I've never heard him before."

"At least one Frank Sinatra song is played at every wedding. It's mandatory," Gray told her. Riya swayed closer to him, in time to the music. The top of her head came up to his chin. It was only because of those killer shoes.

"I like him."

So did he. Especially if it meant that Riya's head was resting on his chest. Her hair smelled like raspberries and some kind of flower. Gray kept his hand resting lightly on her back, tracing the bottom of her tattoo with his thumb.

She shivered.

The song morphed into something from Ed Sheeran, and Riya melted even closer. When was the last time he felt like this?

Never. That was when.

"Loo? Oh, Lieutenant Tyler."

What asshole teammate of mine is interrupting the good thing I've got going on?

Gray looked up and saw Dex grinning at him. That was when he took note of the fact that they were playing some blasted pop song. People were getting their groove on all around them, while he and Riya were lost in their own little bubble.

She looked up at him with a twinkle in her eye. "I think this is our cue to say good-bye to the happy couple and leave." Riya said.

Gray peered over the crowd and laughed at what he saw.

"What?" Riya asked.

He walked them through a throng of dancers ensuring they passed by Mike and Susan. He loved the sound of Riya's laughter as she saw Mike and Susan slow dancing. The newlyweds were lost in *their* own little bubble.

"Still want to say good-bye?" Gray asked.

"I think we can skip it," Riya said, still smiling.

Her laugh was like warm honey.

Oh the things I want to do to this woman.

Gray followed her as she made her way back to the

table. Nobody else was there. She picked up her purse and he put her coat over his arm and they headed out the hotel ballroom to the lobby.

Gray helped Riya into her coat, then held the door open for her as they went outside to wait for the valet to bring up his SUV. Even next to the heat lamp, he saw Riya shiver.

"I have heated seats," he said.

"That's nice." She pressed next to him and snuck an arm around him. Gray hoped it was more than just for shared body heat. He looked down at her, but her head was bowed, so he couldn't get a read on her.

The car pulled up and he helped her inside.

THE SEAT WARMERS weren't nearly as nice as snuggling up to Gray had been. Riya watched him as he concentrated on the road. The rain had turned into a heavy mist.

"I'm glad you're driving."

He kept his eyes on the road, but she saw his smile.

"Why do you say that?"

"This is not my favorite weather condition. I end up driving like an old lady, with my chin up on the steering wheel and people whizzing by me."

Gray barked out a laugh. "You sound like Aunt Jeannine. She's about your height. Please tell me you don't drive a nineteen-eighty-five Buick Regal."

"What color?"

This time Gray did turn his head in astonishment, before quickly turning back to the road.

"I'm kidding. I'm kidding. I drive a Prius."

Riya saw his look of relief. "Do they even have parts for a Buick Regal anymore?" she asked.

"Oh yeah they do. I have to go over to the wrecking yard to get them, but Oz keeps them on hand for me so that I can do repairs when I get back to Springfield."

"You work on your auntie's car?" Riya asked.

She was going to melt into a puddle right here in the passenger seat, and it had nothing to do with the heated seats.

"I'll have to tell Aunt Jeannine that you called her Auntie, she'll love that. She and Aunt Kristie will also get a kick out of Hope's antics at the wedding."

"How often do you talk to them?" Riya asked.

"At least once a week."

"And how often do you visit?"

"Not often enough. I try to get out there for at least a week a year, and then an odd weekend here and there. They're both in their late sixties. Their health is great. Hell, they could run circles around most Marines. Not a SEAL, but a Marine, for sure."

"Don't let Mike or Susan hear you say that," Riya warned.

"Haven't you figured out that giving shit to the other branches of the military is standard operating procedure?"

"They didn't say that in the books I read. But I learned a lot about BUD/S, Jump School and Sniper Training. I read up on a whole lot of the missions that SEALs have been on. I'm surprised so much information is out in the public domain."

Gray's hands tightened on the wheel. "No kidding," he snarled.

"Gray?" she asked. When he didn't answer, she continued to probe. She hated unanswered questions, especially if she thought she'd made someone mad by asking one. "What has you so upset?"

"I don't have a problem with some of those books and articles, but some of them are out of line. They describe too many of our covert ops in detail, and end up giving away privileged techniques and tactics that have kept men safe and innocents alive."

"So how did your teams end up combating this?" she asked curiously.

As he stopped at a light, Gray turned his head and gave her a slow smile. "I like you Dr. Patel. I like you a lot."

She wondered just how high of a temperature those seats went up to, because he sure made her feel warm and good inside. "Well, at least you didn't snarl when you said that. I'll put that into the plus column," she teased. "Tell me why you like me." She couldn't believe how daring she was being.

"I like how smart you are. You immediately understood that we would have a counter-strategy in place."

"Of course you would. You're highly trained special operatives. If you didn't, you'd be stupid and foolish. Nothing about you, Dex or Griffin strike me as low on brain cells."

"You have us figured out. Ergo, I like you."

The light turned green and he continued inland where the fog had lifted. Gray took his right hand off the steering wheel and tangled his fingers with hers. His touch was as magical as his compliments. She stared up into the night sky, ensconced in warmth and peace. The sight of bougainvillea climbing across a long line of fencing roused her out of her reverie. Riya opened her mouth to tell him to turn onto the unlit side street, but Gray already had his blinker on. Yep, the man had it going on.

Gray rubbed his thumb over her pulse as he pulled up to the curb and turned off the car.

"You awake, Princess?"

She rolled her head against the leather seat so she was looking into Gray's blue eyes. "Yes. Do you want to come in for some coffee?"

He hesitated. "I want to, but I have to go into the office tomorrow and clear out some paperwork."

"Oh." Was that her voice sounding so disappointed?

"Also, if I go into your home, we'll be on your couch for hours."

Riya's body clenched at the thought, then her mind clicked in. "I was only offering coffee."

"Riya, you fascinate me. We would end up talking for hours. Then there's this."

Gray turned in his seat and cupped her cheeks. She shivered at the feel of his big hands gently holding her. His thumb feathered against her bottom lip, teasing and tempting her to open. She parted her lips, and swiped her tongue against his flesh.

"Do that again," Gray demanded hoarsely.

Riya's eyes drifted shut and she sucked his thumb into her mouth, loving the warm, salty and exotic flavor that was Gray. When he groaned she looked up at him from beneath her lashes.

His expression could have been pain or pleasure, but the way one hand started pulling the pins from her hair so he could weave his fingers through it, she guessed it was pleasure.

"Enough," he finally muttered. Just the sound of his deep voice had heat coiling low in her body and she was twisting in her seat. Riya yanked at her seatbelt. It wouldn't come off.

"Easy," he said.

He slowly trailed his fingers down from her temple to her chin, then tapped the end of her nose, making her smile. Gray undid her seatbelt and pulled her closer. For once her mind shut down. She didn't care how he'd made so much room between the steering wheel and his body, she was just happy she could settle sideways onto his lap. He made quick work of the sash that was keeping her trench coat closed.

"I've been waiting over a week for this," he said gruffly. His hand slid inside her jacket and touched the bare skin of her back, bringing her closer to him. She felt her nipples pebble against the silk of her dress and Gray slid his chest back and forth against her. She moaned at the sensation.

"Gray, why aren't we going inside?" she whined.

"If we do, it'll go too far. We're still in the get-to-know-you stage."

He wasn't making any sense, but her foggy brain didn't want to figure out the puzzle. She was too busy focusing all of her attention on the rasping sensation.

"I don't care that you're confusing. Just kiss me."

She gripped the short strands of his white-blond hair and pulled down his head so she could feel his lips on hers.

Soft.

Hard.

Demanding.

Coaxing.

Gray was everything. He plundered, and his tongue plunged into her mouth. Her fingers lost their grip, instead her arms twined around his neck and held on for dear life as she went liquid in his arms. So much sensation as Gray swirled his tongue against hers, lighting up nerves she never knew she possessed.

Vaguely she heard a whimper as her hair rippled down her back and he pulled at it, another riot of sensation in her scalp that added to the brilliant feelings that had her rocking her body against his. She was startled when she felt his bold erection pressed against her bottom, but then she felt a sense of pride to think that she evoked such a reaction from a man as strong as Gray.

He tugged on her hair and lifted his head. "Stop squirming, or we're going to be arrested for indecent exposure."

"Sorry, I didn't mean it." All sense of pride and pleasure fled.

"Hey, I've enjoyed every minute, don't you doubt that. I love your reactions, they're beautiful. I just need a minute to get myself under control. You pack quite the punch."

Riya smiled and pressed her forehead against his chest. She took a deep breath. Then another.

"Come on, let's get you inside," he finally said.

"Thought that was too much of a temptation," she whispered weakly into his shirtfront.

He smoothed his hand over the smooth black silk of her hair, then threaded his fingers through it and pulled softly so she would look up at him.

"Sassy. I like it." He kissed her, his lips such a pleasure and provocation. The kiss ended far sooner than she wanted and somehow she found herself resting against the passenger seat. Riya looked at the fogged windows as Gray's door slammed. In a blink she felt the rush of night air washing over her as Gray opened the passenger door. He caught one of her hands and plucked her purse from the floor at her feet and handed it to her.

Riya was thankful for his warmth as his arm wrapped around her shoulders as he led her up to her door. Gray withdrew her house keys at the same time her hormone-muddled brain remembered he had them.

He pushed open the door and stared into her eyes. "Dr. Patel, when can I see you again?"

Riya thought through her schedule. It was hellish for the next week, she planned to work twelve and fourteen hour days. "Anytime you want," she answered.

"Riya, didn't you say you had a presentation due at the end of the week?"

"Oh yeah, I did. So I was right, anytime this week is fine."

Gray's laughter rang out through the night. One big hand slid under her hair to caress the nape of her neck, his other arm wrapped around her waist and drew her close. She had just a moment to see his blue eyes gleam before his mouth covered hers. A tidal wave of pleasure swamped her. Riya closed her eyes and savored the long moments. When Gray finally lifted his head she couldn't help the whimper of loss.

"Wednesday night then?"

She nodded her head.

"Now go inside and I'll wait until I hear you lock the door and you tell me you've set your alarm."

Riya shook her head to clear it. She stroked her fingers over his chest. "Wednesday," she agreed with a small smile. She stepped over the threshold. "I promise to lock up."

"And set your alarm," he reminded her.

"I don't have an alarm."

Gray's expression froze. "Riya, your townhome is the last one on the block and butts up against a small park. Nobody would notice if somebody climbed your back balcony, or jumped up to your bedroom."

Riya leaned against the doorframe and frowned in confusion. "This is one of the safest neighborhoods in the nation. I'm fine."

"And everyone in your life lets you get away with that bullshit thinking?"

"What are you talking about? My parents, sisters, and even Anika's husband didn't say anything about an alarm system, and he's kind of controlling. They were just impressed that I could buy my own home at such a young age." She didn't mention that Anika's husband had made disparaging comments about a single woman buying a home.

"I don't care how safe your neighborhood is, you need an alarm system."

"Hey, wait a minute. How do you know about the park and where my bedroom is?"

"Because I did a recon before knocking on your door today. I wanted to check out the safety of your place."

She laughed. She finally got it. "It's a SEAL thing. You're trained to think about bad guys." She stepped back out onto the porch, and wrapped her arms around him. He held her close. "Gray, the world isn't always a bad place."

He put his knuckle under her chin so she looked him in the eye. "It isn't rainbows and unicorns either."

"I know. It's someplace in between. I really do know that," she assured him.

"Good. I'm glad to hear it. So let's talk about an alarm system."

"But, Gray, there's another part of me that believes if you think the worst scenario is going to happen, that you're just attracting those bad events into your life."

His eyes turned upwards. She knew he was looking to the heavens for strength and she stifled a giggle. If they really started dating she predicted some conflicts ahead. It sounded like fun.

When he looked down, she was caught in his blue gaze.

"I suppose you like Ralph Waldo Emerson, too?" he asked.

She pushed away from him and clapped her hands in glee. "You know the quote! 'Once you make a decision, the universe conspires to make it happen.'

See, if I were to believe in the bogeyman, the universe would send me a bogeyman."

Gray grabbed her hands and pulled her back to him. "You got it wrong. Never believe in the bogeyman, believe in a hero. Just put systems in place to keep you safe. But always believe in the hero. They're out there."

Riya trembled. She was beginning to believe.

5

RIYA'S EYES WERE ALIGHT WITH PLEASURE, AS THEY wound their way around the motel swimming pool, past the Tiki bar. Gray couldn't have asked for anything better, except maybe not so many men staring at her. He'd told her to wear something warm since they were going to be outside at night, so she was wearing a pink angora sweater and black jeans. He'd almost swallowed his tongue when he'd gone to pick her up.

"How did you find out about this place? I mean a drive-in movie, sure. But a pool party movie at a sixties-style motel?" She continued to turn her head every which way, trying to take everything in.

Gray sat down first in the double-seated plush papasan chair, then he reached for Riya so he could arrange her close to him.

"Gray, people are actually swimming," she whispered into his ear.

"Riya, the pool is heated," he whispered back to her. Damn, she was cute. It was the fourth date he'd taken her on, and he found himself enjoying their time together more and more. The woman had a heart as big as all outdoors. She considered herself an outsider because of her intelligence, but she really wasn't. If he had to guess, the way she was raised and educated hadn't allowed her to socialize as much as most people so she struggled a little more. But when she caught onto something, look out.

"You still haven't told me what movie we're going to see."

"It's a surprise."

As they'd walked through the motel lobby, he watched as she looked for some kind of indication as to what the movie was. Surprises were not high on his little scientist's list. She liked to figure everything out. That was part of the reason he'd chosen such a silly movie for them to watch. Okay, maybe not silly, it was one of his favorites after all.

The waiter came over with the drinks and appetizers that he'd pre-ordered.

"Do you need a blanket?" the young man asked.

"I brought one," Gray answered.

"Boy scout," Riya accused with a whisper.

Gray chuckled. "Nope, you got it all wrong. I was an Eagle Scout."

She rolled her eyes. The waiter set the food on the ottoman in front of them. "Oh my God, this looks phenomenal. She eyed the little teriyaki shrimp, and popped one in her mouth. "What kind of drinks are these?" She picked up the coconut with the straw and umbrella.

"They're Mai-Tais."

"I'm going to like this," Riya curled her legs under her, and leaned into him. "This is the life. Just please tell me we aren't watching something scary."

"You don't like scary movies? I would have thought they would be up your alley. You could spend the entire time figuring out who the bad guy is."

"One time Anika was taking care of all of us when my parents went out to dinner. They stayed out really late, and she let us stay up and watch the Exorcist. I had bad dreams for years afterwards."

"How old were you?" Gray frowned.

"I was probably four or five. It was before I started kindergarten. I have never heard my Dad yell like that. He is one of the most easy-going people in the world. He's a surgeon, but people say he has a wonderful bedside manner. Anika was grounded for weeks."

Gray put his arm around her, loving the way she snuggled up close to him. "You have nothing to worry about, even the scary parts are funny."

"Thank you." She took another sip of her Mai-Tai. "How's your beer?"

"Good."

They watched as more people came in and took their places around the pool. He liked seeing how intently Riya observed every little thing around her. Then she frowned, and opened and closed her mouth twice.

"Spit it out, Honey."

"Do you see that couple?" She pointed surreptitiously at a couple who were easily in their mid-seventies sitting in a cabana.

Yeah, like he'd missed that show.

"They have to be my grandparents' age. And I think he has his hand up her skirt."

"Yep, I think management is going to close the flaps on that cabana pretty soon, or ask them to go up to their room."

He was trying to decipher how she felt about this. There was definite shock.

"My parents have never been this demonstrative. I've only seen them kiss when Dad's given Mom a present or something."

Gray just waited.

"I think I like that better. Well, maybe not the public exhibitionism, but definitely the idea that they are so into one another at that age. But is that really possible?"

"I told you I ended up almost living at the Conway's house when I was growing up. I go over and visit Mr. and Mrs. Conway every time I go to Springfield. They've been together forty years and they're always sitting right next to one another on the couch. I can't imagine *not* seeing Mr. Conway's arm around his wife."

"That would be wonderful." Her tone was wistful.

It would. He'd never realized it, but the Conway's marriage had always been his absolute idea of perfection.

A server came with a tray of food. "We have the Caesar salad, pumpkin ravioli and beef medallions," he said.

"You ordered?" Riya asked Gray.

"They had two choices for dinner. One was vegetarian, but after watching you with that meat lovers pizza, I figured the fillet would be fine."

"You thought right."

"Do you want to put out the blanket, before I set down the tray?" the waiter asked.

"Riya?" Gray queried. When she nodded, he snapped out the blanket and covered both of them. He liked how she snuggled even closer to him. It was a Thursday night, which was the only night *The Princess Bride* was playing. So he had to get Dr. Patel home as soon as the movie was over, or her carriage would turn into a pumpkin.

"The movie is going to start in five minutes, we'll come by with flashlights to clear your plates. Don't worry, we'll be quiet," the server said with a grin.

Gray watched Riya's eyes dart over to the cabana, which had been blocked while they'd been served. The older couple were no longer there. Even in the evening light, Gray couldn't tell if she was disappointed or relieved.

All of the lights around the pool were shut off, which just left the blue lights within the pool glowing. Then the movie started playing against the wall high in front of them. Gray waited to see if Riya would recognize the music, but she didn't. Finally the name of the movie appeared and she clapped her hands.

"I've heard of *The Princess Bride*." She pulled to the side and turned so she could get a good look at Gray. "But why would you want to watch something like this? Isn't it just a fairytale for little girls?"

"I'll tell you what, you watch it, and then tell me what parts I liked."

"That'll be easy," she scoffed.

He remembered the first time he'd watched the movie. He'd been seven years old, Aunt Kristie and

Aunt Jeannine had taken him to the theatre in town. He'd gotten his own tub of popcorn, but he forgot about it as soon as Buttercup came on screen. He'd fallen in love. He loved the sword fight, been scared of the monsters, hid at the torture scene, and laughed himself silly over the silly little man. But it was always Buttercup he remembered.

Years later his aunts had purchased the DVD, and he found that he liked the movie even more. There were so many nuances to it. But it also made him sad, there he had been at seven falling in love, believing in love, and there he was at thirty-one, settling. His relationship with Felicia didn't last much longer after that trip to Springfield.

By the time the waiter arrived to take away their meal, Riya was totally entranced by the movie, and Gray didn't think she even noticed that their food had been removed. She had a wonderful laugh, and he wasn't surprised to see her eyes shimmer with tears as the movie progressed. What did surprise him was how often he found her looking at him. She was good at it too. Half the time he didn't notice her doing it, instead he just felt her eyes on him, and he would turn his head and catch her.

"Oh, Gray," she whispered, as the movie came close to the end. "This is so poignant. It's very funny, but it's really loving."

"Are you sure it's not the two Mai-Tais talking?" he teased. The lights came on. People were all standing up and stretching. He didn't want to leave, Riya was perfectly placed against him. It had taken all of his restraint to not do more than cuddle her, but she had been so engrossed in the movie, he didn't want her to miss a moment of it.

As people began to leave the venue, and get out of the pool, Riya looked questioningly at him. "Shall we go?"

"I should have said you needed to bring a jacket."

"I'll be fine."

Gray moved the blanket and then stood up. He held out his hand. Riya took it and stood up as well. He then wrapped the blanket around her.

"Gray, this is overkill."

"Live with it, Lady."

She rolled her eyes for the second time that night.

Little did she know he was damned tempted to carry her to his vehicle. He hadn't realized just how thin that sweater was, he'd been too busy ogling her in it.

Dammit, it was a rookie mistake.

"Gray, why are you frowning. Are you mad at me?" He realized she was having to walk two steps for his every one, and he was frowning.

Great job, Tyler.

"Honey, let me get you into the lobby of the motel, okay?"

She looked sad. He couldn't stand it, so he stopped. He hated it when he made it hard for her to read him. He put his hands on her shoulders and started to rub them up and down along her arms, trying to get the blood moving. He rested his forehead against hers and smiled.

"I'm mad at myself for not realizing how cold it was going to be at midnight and not insisting you bring a coat. I just want to get you onto those seat warmers as quickly as possible, that's all."

"Seriously?"

"Cross my heart."

She let out a deep breath, her smile huge.

He put his arm around her shoulders, and they walked at a more sedate rate out to his car.

By the time they got buckled into their seats and Gray had them on the eight-oh-five heading North, Riya had yawned twice.

"Have you been working long hours?" he asked.

"Probably fewer hours than you. Wanna compare?"

He chuckled.

"Nope. I've played this game with you before. Why don't you rest? We'll be at your house in thirty minutes."

"But I have some ideas on why you like the movie," she protested. Then she ruined it by yawning again. "Maybe I'll rest my eyes for just a minute."

"You do that, Honey."

She put her hand on the console between the seats and Gray took hold of it. His girl worked too hard.

THE NEXT DAY, Susan handed Riya her caramel macchiato latte. She had a huge grin on her face.

"Please tell me that smile is because you and Mike discovered some fantastic new sex position while you were on your honeymoon that you need me to write up in Dr. Kennedy's study," Riya begged.

Miranda laughed. "You should be so lucky. Susan's smile was definitely directed your way."

Susan laughed as she sat down next to Miranda on the small office couch. Both women started sipping their coffee drinks, trying not to smirk.

"I saw that!" Miranda crowed. "You smiled."

"Yep, I saw it too," Susan concurred. "It was a dreamy smile. It was all man-smarmy."

"It was not," Riya denied. "It was the kick of caffeine."

"Bullshit. You were thinking of Gray," Miranda said. "How many dates have you been on now?"

Riya cleared a tiny spot on her desk where she could rest her coffee. The desk was covered in binders, with precise tabs. They were all live projects, otherwise they would be in the overflowing bookcase.

"Come on, 'fess up," Susan pleaded. "I was out of the loop while Mike and I were in Cancun, and then I was stuck playing catch-up. I want all the dirt on you and Gray."

"Didn't you hear? Gray and I broke up after he and three of his team members came over and installed an alarm system without my permission."

Miranda let out a big laugh.

Susan looked between the two of them, confused.

"Don't let her bullshit you. That was a couple of weeks ago. She might have been pissed, but she continues to go out with Gray. I believe their latest date was last night," Miranda said smugly.

"Anyway, Griff told me how unsecure your place was. He would have done the same thing if it had been me," Miranda said.

"So this is getting serious?" Miranda asked gently. It was unlike her, usually she was the more in-you-face type of girl.

"Five," Riya smiled.

"Have you done the deed?" Susan asked point blank.

"Last week he mentioned that he would really like to show me Northern California, maybe take me for a weekend up in Sonoma." She squirmed in her seat just thinking about it.

"He sounds like Griff, he's taking it slow because you matter." Miranda gave a knowing nod.

Susan gave a long-suffering sigh. "Dammit, Mike was the same way. What is with these men?"

"I thought I was just giving off the vibe that I wasn't all that experienced, so he was taking it slow."

"Just how experienced are you? I thought you were a virgin." Susan said.

"I'm not the most experienced girl in the world, but no, I'm not a virgin," Riya defended herself. Dammit, she was blushing.

Susan opened her mouth to ask another question, but Miranda cut her off. "Enough, if she wanted to share, she'd share." Miranda paused. "How do you feel about him?"

"I've never had someone so attentive. He opens doors. He always helps me into my coat. He even holds out the chair for me at dinner. He told me it was a Southern thing."

"Oh no, it's a Military thing," Susan said. "But Mike doesn't hold the chair out for me at dinner."

"Neither does Griffin," Miranda said. "But I never

72

get to go down the stairs first. He always worries about my safety, so he wants to make sure that if I lose my footing he'll be able to catch me."

Riya's eyes widened. "I noticed that Gray did that, but I never realized why."

Miranda's mobile phone chirped and she frowned. "It's the director's ringtone. Gotta go." She took the additional napkins that Susan proffered and started out of Riya's office as she answered her phone.

"So, are you going to go up to Sonoma with him?" Susan asked Riya.

Riya's cell phone rang. She looked down at the display. She recognized it as a number from the Pentagon. "Susan, I need to take this. Let's talk later, okay?"

"Understood," her friend smiled as she left her office.

"Hello, this is Dr. Patel," Riya answered.

"Dr. Patel, this is Colonel Lockhart. We have a situation. We need you in a briefing tomorrow morning here in Washington."

THE LIGHTS WERE OFF in the room and all of the members of Black Dawn were looking at the photograph of a young woman with clear hazel eyes and brown hair pulled tightly back from her face. Gray wondered what she would have looked like if she'd smiled.

"Brief us," Gray commanded his youngest team member, Wyatt Leeds.

"This is Emily Hoag, she's twenty-four and the youngest daughter of Leland Hoag, the American Ambassador to Oman. She's been the tutor to two minor Saudi princes for the last nine months."

Another slide came up, and a dazzling blond woman appeared on screen. She could easily have been a super model or movie star.

"This is Chantelle Briggs, she has been the mistress of Prince Khalid bin Al Halabi for the last two years. He's in charge of the Greater Dammam Investment Bank," Wyatt explained.

"Define 'in charge'," Dex demanded.

Gray was interested to see how Wyatt would handle this question considering Dex was normally in charge of gathering all the intelligence for Black Dawn. With Wyatt's injury on one of the last missions, Dex had been training him on intel and communications. Gray knew Dex was now putting Wyatt through his paces.

"Khalid bin Al Halabi is a minor prince and a distant cousin to the ruling Saudi king," Wyatt said. "Therefore he gets to run the day-to-day operation, but the Saudi royal family owns the bank, and that's who bin Al Halabi reports to."

"So break down what happened," Gray requested.

"Three days ago, bin Al Halabi and his two sons who are fourteen and sixteen years old, and two bodyguards were rushed to a private hospital of the royal family in Al Khobar. The fourteen-year-old, Mohammed, was close to death. His older brother wasn't doing much better. Khalid was in and out of consciousness." Wyatt projected a picture of an Arab man with his arm around two teenage boys who looked remarkably like him.

"The five males, Ms. Hoag and Ms. Briggs were all staying at the royal villa at the Al Khobar Beach Resort. We know this because one of the doctors at the private hospital is Australian, and he has been secretly providing the United States Saudi Ambassador with information. All five of the Saudis were suffering from what looked like late stages of meningitis. In the notes that the Australian doctor provided, it said that Ms. Hoag told the emergency crew the symptoms came on suddenly. Poisoning was suspected. All of the food in the suite was inspected."

"The women weren't affected?" Aiden O'Malley asked the obvious question. He was Gray's second-in-command.

"Not according to what our source was told." Wyatt answered. "The women haven't been seen or heard from since the bin Al Halabis and his men were hospitalized. Emily's father hasn't brought in the media at this point. He knows the drill."

"So the Saudis are just assuming that the women were responsible?" Hunter Diaz asked Wyatt.

Gray watched as Wyatt hesitated. He also saw Dex stop himself from jumping in to answer.

Good.

He wanted to see Wyatt stand up on his own in the communication's role. It was important that he prove to himself that he could bring something of value to the team until his leg healed. Gray was in no doubt that Wyatt would eventually make a full recovery, but in the meantime the young SEAL needed to pull his weight in other ways.

"Hunter, I was informed that the US Ambassador to Saudi Arabia has talked to the Saudi king, but as far as I know, the Saudis haven't come out and said that they think the women are responsible."

"But they've got the women locked up," Hunter pressed.

"I was briefed by the CIA. They told me that right now we're being stonewalled. The Saudi Kingdom is saying the women are being detained for their safety. Our people think that the women are being held by Khalid bin Al Halabi's people and awaiting instruction from him when he recovers."

"Bullshit, they're being 'questioned'," Aiden O'Malley said with air quotes.

"That was my CIA liaison's take as well," Wyatt agreed. "We've got to get them the hell out of there. ASAP." Wyatt was pressing down on the top of his leg. Gray wondered if it was real pain, or if it was a way for him to cope with anxiety.

"So these women have had three days of special attention. Is it likely that either one of them is responsible for the poisoning?" Aiden asked.

"Langley has been through their backgrounds with a fine-toothed comb and came up empty. There's nothing," Wyatt answered.

"I'm not saying it matters, we'll deal with it when we get them out of there," Aiden continued.

"Now I'm up," Gray said. He began to man the projector. A map of the Middle East appeared. "We're heading to Bahrain," he said.

"NSA Bahrain? The Fifth Fleet? I'm taking extra MRE's with me," Dalton Sullivan grumbled. Gray knew Dalton was trying to lighten the mood a little after thinking about the women being tortured.

Dex laughed. "Considering we've eaten rats, snakes and bugs to stay alive, it amazes me you're still freaked out that they served you camel."

"We've had to ride camels. It'd be like eating a horse. No thank you." Dalton shook his head. "I'm sticking to the MRE's."

"You've turned into a pansy ass. If you were married to Evie that wouldn't have happened," Aiden said, shaking his head sadly.

"Ah hell, Mr. Health Food was like that even before Aurora fell at his feet," Dex laughed.

"Listen up," Gray pointed to the map projected up on the wall. "We're not going to have time for a meal at the air base, so problem solved. We're getting our asses over to Um Al Nasan as soon as we touch down. We've got lots of opportunities for things to go sideways, if you catch my meaning." He looked around the room and his men nodded. They all knew that this was not going to be an easy mission.

Gray really wished that he'd worked with any of the leadership at NSA Bahrain. He hated it when he had to rely on people he didn't personally know, especially on a mission that was going to be so fucking complicated. He brought up a satellite image that encompassed the coast of Bahrain and the coastal city of Al Khobar.

"We need to cross this bridge." He pointed to King Fahd Causeway.

He looked at his men. They all had their game faces on.

"Do we have a plan?" Aiden finally asked.

"The commander master chief at NSA Bahrain got his trident twenty-five years ago."

"He must be ancient," Wyatt mumbled.

"For God's sake Leeds, thank fuck you're not going with us. You'd get your ass kicked for sure." Dex shook his head.

"As I was saying, our brother SEAL, Command Master Chief Baker is working on a plan to get us over to Al Khobar. Meanwhile, the diplomatic corps in Saudi Arabia is doing their best to determine if the women are still being held at the Al Khobar Beach Resort, or if they've been moved."

"What is the status on the boys, are they going to live?" Aiden asked.

It was a damn good question. If they died, there was a good chance that they would stop questioning the women and would kill them instead.

"According to Langley, there has been improvement every day, and the fact that their father is regaining consciousness was a great sign for the boys," Wyatt answered.

"Our transport will be taking off in forty-five minutes. I know you brought your go-bags. Make your phone calls, stock up on gear, and have your asses on the plane in forty."

Gray watched as each man left.

Of course Aiden stayed behind.

"Shouldn't you be calling Evie?" Gray asked.

"Already did," Aiden said.

"What are you? Psychic?" He was only partially kidding. When it came to his wife, Aiden was eerily connected to her.

Aiden rested against the desk where the projector sat. They looked at each other in the dim room.

Aiden arched his eyebrow. "Are you calling Riya?"

"Why would I do that?"

"It goes like this," Aiden enunciated slowly. "When a boy starts dating a girl, sometimes he has to leave town. When that happens, he does not leave the girl hanging so that she imagines he has lost interest, or God forbid, he has started dating someone else."

"Or that he is an asshole who has blown her off." Gray said sarcastically.

Gray hid a grin as Aiden winced.

"Yeah, definitely don't follow in my footsteps. I was a total fuck-up," Aiden admitted. "There's one other reason you need to call Riya."

"Do tell." Gray crossed his arms over his chest.

"I hate it when we don't have total control over a mission. We're having to depend too much on the higher-ups in Bahrain. I don't want your focus split."

Most of the time Gray forgot that Aiden was a year older than him, and that he had lived a much harder life. It was at times like these that it shone through. It was the reason he had made him his second-in-command.

"Is there anything else, Mom?" Gray asked.

"Nope, that's it."

"Then gather your shit together, and get to the plane. I have a call to make." Gray pulled out his cell phone and watched Aiden walk out of the briefing room.

He smiled as he got ready to press Riya's number. He even had her picture next to it.

Face it, you're totally gone.

He'd snapped the photo on their third date. She hadn't noticed because she was fighting with her cat. Gray loved Einstein, that cat was the only thing that put her off her game. Riya always knew where everything was, except when Einstein decided to hide things from her. Then she was up shit creek. So Gray had a picture of her trying to pull a business card out of Einstein's mouth. Riya was torn between frustration and laughter as she fought, and Gray had a perfect pic for his phone.

Riya picked up on the second ring. "This must be special if I'm getting a call during office hours."

"You're just as bad," Gray countered.

"Hey, I sent you a text yesterday," Riya sputtered.

"Telling me that traffic's bad on The Five and that I should take the Eight-Oh-Five instead, is not what I would consider real live communication."

"It got you to call me back," she snickered.

"It did at that." Gray fell silent.

"Uh-oh. That silence is not sounding good. Well not that it's making a sound, but you get my meaning."

"Yes I do. Everything's fine. It's just that the team and I have to go wheels up in a half hour."

This time the silence was on her end. Finally she said, "This is the scary stuff, isn't it?"

"Not really, this is the stuff I'm trained to do."

"That's right. That's exactly what I've read. For

goodness sakes, you're worth six hundred and fifty thousand dollars in Navy training aren't you?"

"Nah, that's Griff, I'm worth more," Gray relaxed.

"I wasn't sure. Yeah, you might have a longer period of time in the field, but there's also depreciation because you're old..."

"Woman, you are going to be in trouble the next time I see you," Gray rumbled.

Riya's laughter was a balm to his soul. "Promises. Promises."

After her giggles stopped she said quietly into the phone. "You can't promise when you'll be back, can you?"

"No, Honey, I can't."

"Stay safe, Gray. I figured out why you like *The Princess Bride*, so I need you back home soon so I can tell you."

"This I gotta hear." He liked it that she was trying to end the call on a positive note. "I'll miss you, and please for God's sake stay out of trouble."

"I'll stay out of trouble, if you keep your head down, is it a deal?" she asked softly.

"As you wish."

It was hotter than fuck.

Who in their right mind would give a briefing in the back of a truck when they could have done it in the comfort of a conference room back at CENTCOM? Oh yeah, this guy.

Gray hid his disgust as he looked at the acting commander.

Where in the hell had they dug up this dumble-dick, and why had they put him in charge of this op?

Acting Commander Harry Morris had decided to brief the five members of Black Dawn, the six enlisted men from the fifth fleet, and Command Master Chief Baker in the sweltering back of a tarp-covered truck. What kind of stupid-ass move was that? Fucker even had a laser pointer to highlight routes on the map of the King Fahd Causeway. Just how many men had the pompous asshole gotten killed over the years?

"Tyler, you and your men are going to hide in the refrigerated truck that Stark drove over here from Manama," Morris said. "At one-fifty-five a.m., Paris and Slokovich will create a diversion by sideswiping one another on the causeway. At two-oh-five a.m. our man at customs will be expecting the refrigerated truck to be passing through, so they will turn off the x-ray machine, and you will be able to go through customs undetected."

Morris was *very* pleased with himself.

Tyler glanced over at Baker. The high-level enlisted man might lack expression, but he'd been on the SEAL teams for years and Gray knew that he was pissed off. Baker was the man who was supposed to have designed and led this mission. It had to be a big, hairy political mess over at NSA Bahrain for command to have given the op to this acting dumbfuck, who *wasn't* acting.

"I'll go in place of Slokovich," Baker said in a deferential voice. Gray saw Slokovich's look of relief.

Morris frowned. "That isn't the plan. Slokovich will drive one of the vehicles."

Baker opened his mouth again.

"I will write you up for insubordination if you persist in countermanding my authority." Morris' face turned red. Baker closed his mouth and nodded.

Gray looked around to his team members. They all looked calm and comfortable and he appreciated it. That's because they knew he had their back.

"We're going to need to make some alterations to the plan," Gray said quietly.

"What are you talking about? I've determined the course of action." Morris's voice was sharp.

"We're not going to travel in a refrigerated truck. If someone opens it, we can be picked off like sitting ducks. We'll use one of these tarped trucks." Gray looked at the acting commander straight in the eye.

"That's unacceptable. You'll be seen."

"No we won't. You said you had someone manning the customs crossing. If we had a proper diversion. Something big. Then we won't be noticed."

"And just what would you suggest? We bomb the bridge? We have twenty women do a striptease on the bridge?" One of the men from the fifth fleet laughed. "This is not a laughing matter," Morris shouted at the man.

"Nothing of the sort." Gray kept his voice calm. "I'm suggesting that we fill the refrigerated truck with a small amount of explosives and have it ram into the side of the bridge, approximately thirty meters in front of the customs point. This should be done when we're ready to go into the x-ray machine. The subsequent fire will be just the sort of distraction we need to get us across."

"And who is going to want to do this suicide mission with the refrigerated truck?"

"It's not a suicide mission," Baker said. "Not if it's done right. What's more, I should be able to arrange it so the cab of the truck goes over the side of the bridge and I'll just dive into the Gulf. It'll be perfect." Finally, Baker was showing some enthusiasm.

"I don't like it, we're doing it my way." Morris said.

Gray didn't take his eyes off the acting commander, but he felt each and every one of his men sit a little straighter.

"Commander, can we step outside?" Gray asked.

"No. We cannot." The man turned to Gray's team. "I will take command of you men, if your Lieutenant is unwilling to follow orders. Are we clear?"

"We understand the situation perfectly Commander," Aiden O'Malley said. "I suggest you step out of the truck with our Lieutenant." Hunter, Dex, Griff and Dalton all nodded in agreement.

Gray got out of the truck and waited for Morris to follow.

When Morris jumped out of the truck, he hot-footed it over to Gray and shoved his face into Gray's so their noses were almost touching. "You're going too far." His voice was shrill. "I will be informing my Captain, and he will be speaking to your Commander and Captain as well."

"As long as I'm alive to hear about it, that's fine by me." Gray didn't raise his voice, but he didn't whisper.

Morris shoved Gray, who didn't move. "You and

Baker think you're hot shit because you're SEAL's. You're nothing. I can make and break you all day long. We're doing things my way, or you'll be out of the Navy."

"Again, as long as my men live to see another day, everything is good by me." Gray could see Dex over Morris's shoulder. He had his phone pointed at them. He knew that Dex had done some kind of wizard-trick so the thing could record conversations at a long-distance. He'd been recording everything, starting with the grabtastic plan that Morris had laid out to begin with. Dex always wanted to have the team's collective ass covered. Gray liked that about his communications guy.

It was time to egg the asshole on. More fodder for Dex to film.

"You don't have the power to break me, I have friends in high places," Gray taunted.

"You don't have dick." Morris' grin turned sly. "Unless your uncle owns a Senator from Kentucky, you can't do shit. It's great to come from money, you should try it some time. So we're going to do things my way. You got it?"

"Nope, I don't got it. I've decided people are going to live, and then you can go sniveling to Uncle Moneybags about how the SEAL's didn't do what you wanted. I have one question for you though, because I'm curious. Did you even make it through even one day of BUD/S?"

Morris' face turned red, then he spat on Gray's boots. "You SEAL's are pussies."

By the time Morris turned around, Dex had disappeared from the opening of the truck.

6

————

IT DIDN'T FALL TO SHIT UNTIL THEY HIT SAUDI ARABIAN soil. Getting through customs had been a breeze. Baker had performed like a rockstar. It turned out that the inside man at customs had two cousins who worked with him, so the three of them had combined forces to pass Gray and his team through while everyone else was concentrating on the fire on the bridge. It had been beautiful. By the time they reached the resort, Slokovich had notified Dex that Baker had made it safely back to land in Bahrain. But now they were here at the Al Khobar Beach Resort and not even the slightest bit of their intel had turned out to be correct.

"Dex?" Gray asked.

"I'm working on it." His man's eyes never left his computer. They were in the cramped mechanical room that was supposed to have housed the two women. Instead it was crammed full of boilers, air handlers and electrical generators. Two workers were hog-tied and blindfolded in the corner.

Gray so wanted to tell his communications expert to work faster, but that would be useless, because nobody worked faster on a computer than Dex.

Dalton and Griff were checking all of the Villas, while Hunter had the riskier job of checking out the rooms in the interior of the hotel. Gray had dispatched Aiden to check over the Royal Villa where the poisoning had taken place.

It was now four-thirty in the morning. His team knew that they only had fifteen more minutes before they had to reassemble back at the beach.

"Got something," Aiden's voice came over the team's shared receiver.

Dex's eyes never left his computer screen as he continued to search, but Gray knew he was listening to Aiden's words.

Aiden continued, "There's blood in the master bathroom. A lot of it. Rope's hanging from the shower curtain."

Gray's blood ran cold. "So they questioned the women in there?"

"Looks like." Aiden's voice was flat.

"How much blood?" Hunter asked over the com. "Do you think they're dead?"

"No," Aiden answered. "One of them left a message behind the toilet. It's small, but I can make out the word 'gold' and some kind of symbol."

"Describe the symbol to me," Dex said urgently. His fingers slammed the keyboard.

"It's an upside down triangle with two lines in it, and a line coming down from the bottom."

"Time's up. All of you get your asses to the beach," Gray ordered.

"Not me, I've almost got it," Dex said. A bead of sweat dripped down his forehead. Gray went to the door and opened it a crack. The sky was beginning to lighten.

"Forget it, Dex. We're leaving."

"Aiden, you still there?" Dex demanded.

"Yep," Aiden answered.

God fucking dammit.

"Aiden, I told you to get the hell out of there." Gray was going to kill Aiden if he wasn't killed by a bogey.

"What's your question, Dex?" Aiden asked calmly.

"Could the symbol be a tulip? Could the whole thing be Golden Tulip?" Dex demanded.

Gray could actually hear his man's hope. "Absolutely. Does it mean something?"

"You heard our boss. Get your asses to the beach," Dex said as he crashed his computer shut and shoved it into his rucksack. He turned to Gray. "Let's go."

"What? Explain it to me." Gray peered out the window of the cabana, then nodded to Dex when he saw the coast was clear. They kept to the shadows until they hit the high wall that separated the beach and the luxury resort. Gray gave Dex a leg up, then hauled his own ass up and over. They were the first to arrive at the rendezvous point.

"Status," Gray demanded. Seconds seemed like hours as he waited for his team to answer. The flavor of the air changed and Gray turned to see Griff and Dalton coming up behind him.

"Goddammit—" Gray started.

"Got a problem." Gray could barely hear Hunter's whisper.

"Need backup?" Gray whispered back.

"Negative." Aiden's voice was tense.

Fuck! Information would really be appreciated at this moment.

Dex had his comp out again, Gray saw the satellite image up on his computer. He was trying to focus in on the royal villa.

A gurgle came through the receiver. Aiden answered the unasked question. "One tango down."

"Guys, there's a total of eight in the villa," Dex said quietly. "That makes six bad guys and you two mugs."

"Five now," Aiden's voice was almost soundless.

"Make that four," Hunter whispered. A light thud came through the receiver. "Oopsie, now there's only three."

When the hell did Diaz turn into such a smartass?

Silence.

Gray looked down. Even in the moonlight he could see the individual grains of sand on the beach, the Navy appreciated his perfect eyesight.

He started counting, willing his men to be all right. To be safe.

Gray flinched as a rifle shot went off with a muffled roar.

He heard more shots. He wanted a report. Damn it, he wanted to know what was going on. Listening intently, Gray tried to imagine what was playing out in the villa. It was definitely his guys doing the shooting, but then he heard another volley of shots from farther away.

Still no sound from Aiden or Hunter.

That was good news. There would have been a very familiar thud / grunt that would have come through if their body armor had been hit. Gray refused to even think about the sound any other type of accurate shot could have made on his men's flesh.

Goddammit. I want a report!

He looked up from the sand and his gaze caught Dalton's.

Was that a smile of reassurance on his friend's face?

Christ, these men fell in love and they all changed. Maybe he should talk to his commander about doing a fitness for duty report each time a team member got engaged or married. A picture of Riya flashed before his eyes. He scowled and focused harder on the silence in his earpiece.

"We got 'em. We're on our way." Aiden said in a normal voice.

Halleluiah.

"He's a geek at heart," Aiden murmured as he sidled up next to Gray.

"Nope, he was born and bred to be a SEAL," Gray disagreed.

"But he has a unholy relationship with his computer, you have to admit that. Where most of us would sleep with our knife, he probably sleeps with his comp."

"I can hear you, you know. And, O'Malley, I sleep with my wife." Dex didn't look up from his computer.

"See, he's got the supersonic hearing of a geek," Aiden said quietly.

"SEAL's have the highly-developed hearing of a SEAL, thank you very much. Just because you and Gray are so old you don't understand technology, don't take it out on me."

Gray heard Griff and Dalton smother their laughter, which is just what Aiden had been aiming for. Tension had been high as they had slowly headed North toward the King Abdulaziz Seaport for a good part of the day, only to find out they were headed in the wrong direction. Thank God Dex had been able to ferret out where the Golden Tulip was actually docked.

"I still can't believe they've named the place Dana Beach on Half Moon Bay. Do they like California much?" Griff asked.

"Who gives a shit what they call it, as long as we're finally here," Hunter said. Gray could tell his patience was shot. But then he heard Hunter take a deep breath. *Good man.*

Gray watched as Hunter's lip ticked up. "You know, I just took Aliana to a jazz concert at Dana Point about three weeks ago." He waved his hand to gesture across at the gated four-star resort that looked like a dilapidated Holiday Inn in the middle of the Mojave Desert. "Even she would burst out laughing if she were to compare the two places."

"So how good is the intel?" Dalton asked Dex.

"That's definitely the Golden Tulip," Dex pointed to a yacht that was out past the harbor. It wasn't in sniper range. "It belongs to Prince Khalid bin Al Halabi's brother-in-law."

"How are they related?"

"His wife's brother," Dex answered Dalton.

"That takes balls." Hunter shook his head. "This guy really arranged to hold his mistress hostage on his wife's brother's yacht?"

"From what our friend Kane told me, Faizon, the brother-in-law, is one twisted fuck. Not only would he be happy that his sister's rival is being hurt on his turf, he'd also like to be in on it."

"You called McNamara?" Gray asked. He was surprised that Dex would have reached out to the communications expert on the Night Storm SEAL team, since they'd only worked together once before.

"Nope, Wyatt did," Dex answered with a shit-eating grin. "Wyatt got Kane doing a lot of the deep background research for him ever since I pinpointed the yacht," Dex's voice full of admiration. "My little boy is growing up. He figured out a way to get someone else to do his work for him." Dex pretended to wipe a tear from his eye.

"Can the shit," Gray grimaced. "We get it, Wyatt did good."

"Damn right he did," Dex said. "Kane is fucking connected, he sure knows how to forage for gossip."

"I don't know, I still think you're the biggest gossip in the fifth fleet," Dalton drawled.

Dex shot him the bird.

Gray snorted, Dalton was right. It was like the pot calling the kettle black. If the situation weren't so hellish, it would be fun to see Dex so jazzed. He had schematics, gossip and was ready to grip a knife in his teeth and swim out in the harbor and rescue the two women.

Gray took a moment to look around at the rest of his men. Griff was the perfect SEAL, he was anything Gray needed him to be. There wasn't a damn area he didn't excel in, but water was his home. He'd definitely be going out to the yacht.

Hunter was trying to keep it low-key, but his need for retribution was second only to Aiden. The man was off-the-charts protective. Gray shifted his attention to his second-in-command. He'd been damn near mute since finding the evidence of torture in the bathroom. Gray thought back to when Aiden's wife Evie had been captured in Turkey. It had been through sheer force of will that he'd kept it together and saved his woman, but he'd done it. Yep, Aiden had managed a miracle and tonight wouldn't be any different. His whole team were going to work miracles for these two women.

"Gather round children, I have a plan," Gray smiled.

GRAY HAD DRIVEN the truck a mile south of the Dana Beach Resort and hid their truck behind an abandoned house. Dex had somehow scoped out a dock that they were going to eventually bring the women back to. This was where the plan got a little...flexible.

Kane had tracked down the former captain of the Golden Tulip. The man had only lasted seven weeks after Faizon bought the yacht, but it was enough time for the older Saudi to have intel regarding the security setup. He was also the one who gave Kane the scoop on just what a sick and paranoid fuck Faizon was.

"Here's where they're weak," Dex pointed to the stern of the yacht. "Four open decks for people to get skin cancer, and for us to climb aboard. According to the captain, they only ever had guards on the lower and main decks, never on the upper deck. Doubt it's changed."

"What kind of artillery are the men using?" Aiden asked.

"Kane said that from the description they were submachine guns. More than likely MP5K's. The captain said that Faizon always travels with a security detail of twelve. They're all former military, tough sons of bitches."

"So the captain saw them in action?"

"Yep. They took down two boats of Somali pirates. That wasn't the problem. It was when there was a party on board, and the Cap realized that some of the female guests weren't allowed to leave. A girl jumped overboard in the Mediterranean Sea. One of the guards gunned her down. The captain hid. He didn't want anyone to realize that he had witnessed the killing." Everyone stared at Dex in silence.

"I know, harsh shit, isn't it?" Dex said quietly.

"What about the other girls?" Hunter finally asked.

Dex's shoulders hunched, then he looked up and stared his friend Hunter in the eye. "He never saw them again. At the next port, the captain got off the ship for supplies and never came back."

"How'd Kane track him down?" Gray asked.

"Fuck if I know, he's as good as Clint Archer," Dex

said. Hell, that was high praise. Clint Archer was the communications and intelligence guru from Midnight Delta. Dex had worked with him for years.

"Where's Clint?" Hunter asked.

"The Midnight Delta team is in Nigeria."

"Shit," Griff breathed.

They all nodded.

"Fucking Boko Haram. Nigeria is the worst. You're stuck fighting against women and children who've been kidnapped and brainwashed. It's heartbreaking," Aiden said bitterly.

Gray looked at his men. "Okay, enough of their shit, we've got our own to worry about. We need to get to those two women before they're thrown into the Persian Gulf." He nodded at Dex who was kneeling in front of his comp. "You're staying here and coordinating everything. We'll let you know as we dispatch the bad guys. Did your know-it-all new best friend have any idea how many people besides the guards are on the yacht?"

"Faizon and his family. That would be his grown son, and two teenage daughters."

"He took his family? Two young daughters?" Gray felt his stomach turn over.

"I just pray to God he's keeping his daughters far away from what's going on with his prisoners," Aiden said. Gray remembered one of the human trafficking missions Aiden had worked on with the Midnight Delta team. The people involved had been evil.

"Okay, we want to hit the yacht at two a.m. We want off the boat at two-thirty, and no more than an hour after that, I want our asses back on the truck with the women, headed for Bahrain." All of his men nodded.

"Aiden, did you take what you needed for triage?" Gray asked. Aiden was one of the best medics he knew.

"I'll do what I can on the yacht," Aiden assured him. "Dalton, you know the drill."

Dalton nodded. As the leanest man on the team, he would be giving up his wetsuit to one of the women. Dex's wetsuit would be carried by Griff because extra weight wouldn't slow him down.

"Do a communications check," Dex demanded.

They all checked their mics and receivers, then dropped into the water off the dock. Gray was the last to go in. If anything happened to one of his men, he'd be there to take care of them and haul their ass back to shore. But with these Navy SEAL's, seeing the sun at midnight would be more likely. Still, it was his job to have their six.

7

THE ONLY SOUND THAT COULD BE HEARD WAS THE lapping water of Half Moon Bay. Gray watched as Griff silently undid the chain at the bottom of the staircase that lead from the water up to the main deck of the Golden Tulip. Then he started climbing the stairs.

God, could they make it any easier?

Gray, Griff and Dalton had all spotted the guard at the top of the stairs as they swam toward the starboard side of the yacht. He was peering into one of the windows of the boat, instead of watching over the rail or toward the stair.

Dalton was next up the stairs after Griff. He stayed low, so that only one member of Black Dawn could be seen above the main deck if the asshole guard actually turned around...which he didn't. Griff took his knife out and silently killed the man, then Dalton rushed up to help Griff prop the body up against the side of the wall so it would look like the dead man was sleeping.

Aiden and Hunter were at the stern. Their job was

to take out the two guards on the lower deck, then climb up to the main deck and take out those two as well. They still hadn't reported in. When Gray had laid out his plan, Hunter and Aiden had both said, 'piece of cake', at the exact same time. They better not have jinxed themselves.

Gray climbed the stairs where Dalton and Griff were waiting for him.

"Lower deck clear," Aiden's voice came through clearly in Gray's earpiece.

"Climbing up to the main deck," Hunter whispered his report.

"One guard dispatched on port side of main deck," Griff said into his mic. "I'm heading to port via the bow, I'll monitor the interior through the windows and doors as I go. Don't shoot me."

"Roger that." Gray heard Hunter's grin through the receiver.

"Dalton and I will repeat the procedure clockwise." Gray gave a hand signal for Dalton to follow while he took point toward the stern. Gray quickly peered through each window, but when he got to the door, he went down to his stomach and peeked around.

Damn, there was a guard who was actually alert. He was looking up high, though, so he missed Gray. He needed to take him out quietly. He did a sweep of the room, it was an open area with a circular staircase in the middle.

He turned his head and looked at Dalton, raising one finger.

"Get his attention, so the guard comes out to the

deck. I'll dispatch him as soon as he opens the door," Gray whispered into his mic.

Dalton nodded. He padded over to the rail, close to the door, but still out of the guard's line of sight. He took his fin and slapped it against the steel rail. The rapping of the rubber against the metal made a distinctive thwapping sound that had the guard turning to the door, his sub-machine gun at the ready. He spoke into a microphone attached to his shoulder, similar to what police officers wore, then he moved slowly toward the door.

"Dalton, enough," Gray muttered into his mic. "Team, my bogey just called out to his team that he heard something. Your targets might be on the move to the main deck interior staircase."

"Gray, we're on the upper deck, immediately above you. All outside guards are dead, but you're about to have company, two more guards are coming down the stairs. Hunter's staying with the two Saudi girls, I'm going up to the owner's deck," Aiden said.

Gray looked over his shoulder and saw Dalton nod.

"Give me the fatality numbers," Dex demanded from shore.

"Two," Hunter said.

"Two," Aiden said.

"Two," Griff answered.

"Zero," Gray and Dalton answered at the same time.

"But we'll have three in just a second," Gray whispered as the door slowly opened. Gray grabbed the Saudi's ankle and yanked, and in a graceful coordination, Dalton ripped the submachine out of his hands before he could do anything with it. The man hit the deck with a thud. Gray immediately covered the man's mouth, then shoved his knife into the back of the man's neck and twisted. Dalton and Gray dragged him out of the line of sight of the door a millisecond before they heard booted footsteps descending the stairs.

Gray gave a chin tilt to Dalton, who put his back to the wall and started to turn with his MP7, when Gray heard a short blast of gunfire in his receiver and overhead at the same instant.

"Two more down, Dex," Aiden said calmly.

Dalton finished turning and let loose with a hail of bullets. The two Saudi guards were laid out before they could even get a shot off.

"Three," Dalton said into his mic.

"Which means there is one still on the loose," Gray said to his men. "Time to spread out. I want those women found." Gray looked at his watch. "You have fourteen minutes to get off this boat."

"I have the two daughters with me." Hunter said. "They're in good shape," he said before Gray could ask the question.

"I want them secured, and you to help search," Gray commanded. "I'll take the lower and tank decks. Dalton, you take the main deck. Hunter and Aiden, I want your asses up to the bridge, now. We're going to have some nervous crew members up there. I want them secured, and or taken out. That's going to be your call, you'll know their status. That doesn't just go for the crew on the bridge, you got that?"

Gray heard all of his men agree. They knew their jobs.

They'd already been on the lower deck, so Gray

headed straight for the tank deck. He just had a feeling. He'd been around a lot of years, and he'd learned not to discount *feelings*. Gray yanked open the door and went inside, his rubber-soled boot ensured that he didn't slip in the blood as he ran by one of the dead guards. He triple-timed it down the stairs, until he hit the lower deck, then he ran back toward the stern of the yacht. Gray shook his head in wonder. They'd fancified the door to the engine room in fine grain maple, but as soon as he opened the fancy-assed door he was looking into the same old guts of a boat. Bright lights, steel and the smell of grease and motor oil. It was hot and noisy, too. Kind of felt like home.

He slowed the door down so that it shut softly, and then he crouched down beside the left stair rail. He was out in the open, so he tried to make himself a small target in case there were more guards than anticipated, or if the engineer or one of the mechanics had guns. Then there was Faizon or his son. Gray was positive that this was where they were holding the women. He didn't have anything to go by except for instinct. Damn, now he was sounding like Zed.

Oh for God's sake, it's away from the women and soundproof. This is logic, Tyler. Not whoo whoo psychic shit.

Gray crept down the stairs, then shot across the floor two meters so he could hide behind the ship's main oil tank. Damn, how the hell could he smell body odor while he was butt up against three hundred gallons of grease? A man had to be close. Gray waited and listened, and took a deep breath in. Gray's eyes watered.

Yep, real close.

A light footstep. Just the one. He heard the sound of metal touching metal. Gray recognized it, a wrench turning a bolt. He peered just enough around the corner so he could confirm that there was a man in a sweat-soaked dingy white tank t-shirt working on a hydrophore pump.

Gray didn't see anyone else. He rushed him, hitting the mechanic on the back of the head with the butt of his gun. The man was out for the count. Gray still took a moment to search him for any weapons. There was nothing.

There had to be at least an engineer and another mechanic for a boat this size. He remained in a crouch. He was surrounded by tanks and pumps, he needed to get over to the boiler and piston rod. How often had he seen the chief engineer bitching about that equipment? By the sounds of things, he needed to move even farther to the back of the boat. Gray continued to use the large tanks as cover.

He hit pay dirt when he heard two men speaking in Arabic. They were not happy. As Gray got closer he could hear them talking about the woman who was being held in the engine store room. They were debating whether they should give her some water.

Gray stepped out from behind the water cooling tank, his submachine gun pointed at them. The fat man's arms flew in to the air, the second guy stood stock still.

"Hands up," Gray said in Arabic. When the second man still didn't comply, Gray took three menacing steps forward and repeated his command in a lower voice. The man finally held up his hands.

"Turn around, hands on the wall, legs spread." Once again the second man was slow to respond. As soon as he turned around, Gray slashed down with the butt of his weapon between the man's neck and head. He fell to the floor like a bag of wet cement.

He patted down the other man and didn't find any weapons.

"Take off your shirt and your friend's shirt."

The older man stared at him blankly. Gray said it again, slower. The man complied. He handed the grungy cloth to Gray. He really didn't want to touch it. He threw one of the shirts on the floor, then ripped the other one into strips and swiftly gagged and hogtied the unconscious man.

"Where's the women?"

Again with the blank stare.

"Where are the women?" he repeated his question slower. Gray knew he was speaking Arabic fluently.

"Only one woman." The man pointed at a door. "She needs water. She's hurt."

"Take me to her," Gray demanded.

The man stumbled forward, looking over his shoulder at Gray's submachine gun.

"Hurry up."

When he got to the door, he pulled at the key ring attached to his belt and unlocked the door. They were met by silence and darkness.

Please let her be alive.

He shoved the big man to the deck and felt for the light in the little room. He hit the switch, immediately scanning the floor. Which was when he saw her bare, dirty feet dangling in front of him.

Gray grabbed her around her hips, and she moaned.

Thank God that she had moaned, it told him she was alive. He looked up and saw her gaze down at him through swollen eyelids. He couldn't tell the color of her eyes, all he could see was blood where the whites of her eyes should have been.

Gray couldn't tell which woman it was. He looked at her hair. The strands were so dank, matted and sweat-soaked, that he couldn't tell if it was Kelley's brown hair or Chantelle's blond hair.

"Miss, I'm with the United States Navy. I'm going to get you out of here."

They had her tied to one of the pipes that ran across the ceiling. Her hands were swollen and dried blood coated her wrists. Gray pulled out his knife and cut her down. She collapsed over his shoulder, and he laid her gently onto the floor. He put his fingers to her neck. Her pulse was weak.

"Aiden. You got anything?" he growled into his mic.

"Nada," his second-in-command answered immediately.

"Get your ass down to the tank deck. Got one of the women. She's in really bad shape."

"Roger."

She whimpered, it was so low he almost thought he'd imagined it.

"We're going to get you out of here." He saw the incomprehension on her face.

Tenderly he cupped her cheek. "Safe. You're safe now."

"Give me a report," Dex said quietly into his ear.

"I don't know which woman it is. She's bad, Dex."

"Fuck," he heard Griff whisper sadly in his ear.

He watched a tear track down her face.

Gray sprang up and found the man slumped outside the door. He hadn't moved a muscle. When he saw the rage in Gray's face he covered his head with his hands and begged for mercy. "Not me. It wasn't me," he wailed.

"But you knew, didn't you? You heard?"

"Faizon. It was him. Him and his son."

"But you heard," Gray reiterated.

Gray kicked him. Hard. He grabbed the undershirt that was beside the man and ripped it up, quickly gagging and hogtieing him, like he had the other engine mechanic.

"Where is she?" Aiden asked as Gray finished tying the mechanic up.

The big blond man was by his side, and Gray led him inside the room. Aiden was on his knees next to the injured woman before Gray could even blink.

He heard a spurt of gunfire over his receiver. "Found the other guard," Hunter said.

"She's bad," Aiden said. He pulled out a kit from his small waterproof pack. He rolled it out and inserted a needle into a vial, carefully measuring out some liquid.

"Can't give her too much," Aiden muttered to Gray. His friend's eyes told him all he needed to know. She wasn't going to make it if they didn't get her to a hospital...fast.

Gray and Aiden's heads shot up as they heard a woman's screams. Both of them looked at the woman on the floor who was barely conscious, then realized it was coming over their receiver.

"Hunter, get to the upper deck. I'm at the bow. In the most forward cabin. Get here yesterday," Griff ground out. "I've got the Ambassador's daughter."

At least Gray now knew that Aiden was caring for Chantelle.

"Anybody else?" Dex asked.

"Two pukes stupid enough to still be begging for help. They're nothing but corpses, who're taking too long to die."

Griff had never sounded like that before. Never. Aiden's glance snared Gray's. This was not good.

"Hunter, you there yet?" Gray demanded.

"Griff, I'm almost with you," Hunter said, by way of answer. "Keep it together." Gray could hear Hunter Diaz's heavy breathing as he swiftly ran toward Griff and whatever mess he had found.

"What's the status of the girl?" Dex asked Griff.

Good for Dex, get Griff's mind off the two men.

Another scream came over Gray's receiver.

"Ahhh, God," Hunter's voice was anguished.

"Help me," Griff said above the woman's cries.

"Dammit, Hunter. Griff. I want a status now." Gray appreciated how Dex was keeping command of the situation.

"She'll make it," Hunter said.

Who was he reassuring? Griff?

The screaming began to lose volume, but that somehow made it worse.

What the hell was going on?

Gray turned his head and crouched down beside

Aiden. He couldn't do anything about Emily Hoag, so he would concentrate on the woman he *could* help.

"Was the bridge clear?" he asked Aiden.

Aiden gave him a side eye look, then went back to working on Chantelle's hands. He had bandaged her wrists, now he was rubbing circles on her palms, and twining his fingers between hers, trying to restore circulation. Even with the morphine running through her system, she was moaning in pain. But the sounds she was making were nothing compared to the high-pitched shrieks coming from Emily.

"Lieutenant, at your six," Dalton called. Gray heard him in stereo. He stood up and opened the door to the engine store room. He saw his man bent over one of the men Gray had tied up. It looked like he was regaining consciousness. Dalton had picked up some rope in his travels and was attaching the man to one of the pumps.

"Get this guy, too," Gray said, pointing to the guy slumped near the door. Dalton nodded.

"All decks are cleared. We're good to go now that we have the women," Dalton reported as he moved to tie up the next man.

"Dex?" Gray spoke into his mic.

"No can do," Dex answered his question before he posed it. "The only safe way to bring the yacht close to shore is the marina at Dana Beach resort. If you tried going to shore any other way you'd rip out the bottom of the boat. But the resort is out, because it's too crowded. There's a wedding going on, you'll be spotted. Your only option is our initial plan for you to meet up here."

"Aiden, can you stabilize her for the swim back?"

"We don't have to swim," Dalton said as he came into the room. "Since we've overtaken the yacht, it doesn't matter what we do. Normally I'd throw up at the sight of the world's most overpriced lifeboats that I swear have leather seating, but I'm thanking God for them right now for these two ladies."

Gray nodded. "Get them ready."

Dalton nodded and disappeared.

"Did you hear that Griff? Will that work?" Gray asked.

"It'll have to," Hunter answered. "We'll get her there. We're over our time."

"I can't do a fireman's carry," Aiden told Gray. "She has at least two broken ribs."

"You're not carrying her. I am. You need to get up to Griff and Hunter and see what's going on with Emily. I've got Chantelle."

Aiden had his kit packed up before Gray finished talking.

"Guys," Gray said. "Aiden is aiming for the two of you. How can he help?"

There was a pause. Then Hunter whispered. "She needs to be knocked out. She's fighting us. She's out of her mind with fright and I can't blame her. There's not one of us who could talk her down right now after what those animals did to her."

"Are they dead?" Dex snarled.

"Griff took care of them. They're still hanging on. They're going to die bad."

Aiden, Dalton and Dex all said "Good," simultaneously.

Gray picked up Chantelle. "Did you grab the port or the starboard lifeboat?" he queried Dalton.

"Starboard."

"Men, I'm taking Chantelle to starboard. Dalton's with me. The rest of you go to the port lifeboat."

"I'll head there as soon as Aiden arrives," Hunter said.

Chantelle stirred in his arms. "Emily?" she whispered. "Where's Emily?"

"She's alive," Gray assured her as he weaved his way around the different pumps and tanks toward the stairs. He saw tears trailing down her face.

"Hurt," she whimpered.

"I know it hurts, Miss. We're going to get you to a hospital."

Gray juggled with the door knob, and tried to shoulder the door open at the same time she lifted her hand in the air and waved it in front of his face. "Not me. Hurt Emily."

"I've got the boat. It's midship on the lower deck. We'll load up and winch us onto the water.", Hunter said.

"Got it," Gray said. Even though he was walking fast, he did his best not to jostle Chantelle as he made his way up the stairs to the lower deck. He finally heard Aiden with Griff.

"Hold her still," Aiden barked. It had to be a shit situation, but Griff needed to lay hands on the woman in order to help her. Her scream of terror was heartbreaking. "I'll take her," Aiden said after a long moment.

Yep, a shitty situation.

. . .

GRAY'S BOAT was the first one to reach land. He didn't know how he'd done it, but by the time he got Chantelle to the truck, he found that Dex had some of the softest pillows and blankets imaginable.

"Where'd you get these?"

"You don't want to know."

Fuck, no wonder he knew there'd been a wedding at the resort.

Chantelle was unconscious, and her breathing was labored, but no blood bubbles. Her fingers were pink, so that was a blessing. Gray left her in the truck with Dalton. He was the second best medic on the team.

Hunter and Aiden were pulling the boat to shore. Griff held Emily in his lap. There had only been one time Gray had seen Griff look this broken up, and that was when Miranda had been close to death. Gray waded beside the boat and held out his arms. He saw that she was wrapped up in a bed spread.

"Hand her to me, so you can get out of the boat. Okay?"

"She's so young," Griff said.

"You've done enough. It's time for the rest of us to take care of her. Give her to me, I promise she'll be safe," Gray said.

Griff hesitated only a moment. "I know you will, man. It's just that her eyes are the exact color as Livvie's," he said, referring to his daughter. The blanket slipped as he handed the girl over to Gray. Her soft, naked shoulder was exposed.

Gray's worst fears were confirmed. He gently took the young woman out of Griff's arms, and gave Griff a nod of approval.

Griff sighed. His glance cut over to the big, blond Irishman. "I'm sorry, Aiden."

"Sorry's aren't allowed," Aiden said as he clapped his hand on Griff's shoulder. "I'll take good care of her. Of both of them."

"We need to get them over to Bahrain," Griff said as he walked to shore beside the other men.

"Please tell me we don't have to deal with Dickweed." Hunter said.

"The Dickster had new papers worked up. It was an immediate reassignment to Libya. He's in route right now," Dex said from where he stood at the tailgate of the truck. "Baker is clearing the way for us on our return trip."

"You arrange that?" Hunter asked Dex.

"Nope, it was our boy Wyatt."

Gray felt his shoulders relax. He watched Aiden hand Emily up to Dalton, then he hopped into the back of the truck. Gray turned to look at Griffin Porter.

"Are you—"

Griff waved his hand. "I've got my shit together. Hunter made sure the father and son were dead before we left."

"Good. That's good." No matter how satisfying a long drawn-out gut shot might have been, Gray wanted them dead.

"Everybody good?" Hunter called from the cab of the truck.

"Hold your fucking horses." Dex shoved up the tailgate with one hand. His other cuddling his laptop to his chest. Seriously, it was amazing that

Kenna got pregnant considering Dex's affinity to that thing.

"Livvie has a blanket that she carries around like that," Griff grinned at Gray. "She calls it her dit-dit."

"Dex, what's your computer's nickname?" Gray called out. He could feel even Dalton and Aiden were listening for Dex's answer as he slammed the door to the passenger seat.

"I've heard him call it Honey," Hunter said.

"Damn right I do." Dex's voice was filled with pride. "She's a Honey Badger. This computer has lived through explosions, and has taken down terrorists. She's tough as hell, and doesn't give two shits what you have to say about her, she'll just keep on, keeping on."

Gray loved the sound of his team starting to laugh. He could have sworn that he heard Chantelle give a low snort of laughter.

8

Miranda had said today, that tonight was the night. The men were going to be home. But still nothing. Riya felt like she was going to climb out of her skin. She reached for her moisturizer then set it back down on the nightstand with a thump. Einstein raised his head and blinked.

"Deal with it," she told the cat.

She didn't like this. She wasn't happy, not at all.

She took a deep breath, then another. Better. Not good, but better. At least her skin wasn't itching. It had been eight days since Gray had left on his mission with his team. The longest eight days of her life. She flung back the covers and shoved out of bed. Einstein gave out a half-hearted meow. He was getting used to her scattered sleep pattern.

And here she'd thought that work issues were problematic. She hadn't had a clue. Nothing in her life had prepared her for this.

Riya padded to the bathroom and ran cold water

into the sink. She pushed back her tousled braid and bathed her face. She looked at herself in the mirror. Yep, she still had the bruises under her eyes. It was the days of worry and being scared about something that she had no power over.

"You can't do anything about it, so being upset is useless," she told her reflection.

Yeah, like repeating that again would help.

Einstein rubbed his head against her calf. She blinked fast, her eyes gritty at the thought that her cat was trying to give her comfort.

"You're a good kitty." She looked down at him and wished he was young again so she could pick him up and cuddle him. But he didn't like that anymore.

She continued to stare at Einstein, anything to stop her from looking at herself in the mirror. She didn't want to witness herself falling apart. Riya closed her eyes and rested her hip against the bathroom counter, letting images of Gray float behind her eyelids. Gray's smile, his intense looks, his arms around her, his kisses, him holding her, his breath against her temple, the comfort he provided.

Gray Richard Tyler.

Just Gray.

Please God, let him be safe.

She opened her eyes and stretched her neck, anything to release her tension, trying to figure out how she could be overreacting so badly. She'd been working with Miranda for seventeen months and met Griff more than a few times. She'd watched the two of them play with their daughter. Riya really liked the man. Sure, she'd been concerned when he'd been deployed, but that'd been the extent of it. What's more, Miranda had seemed fine. Surely, Miranda hadn't gone through this kind of torment. Not the bone-wrenching, trouble eating, not sleeping, poison-ivy-itching fear.

Riya leaned forward and rested her head against the mirror. Her breath created fog and she leaned back and watched as her finger drew a heart on the mirror.

"Finish it."

She wrote G.R.T. and R.N.P. inside the heart. Yep, she was over the moon for this man. She was so far past the point of in love...was there a term that was more encompassing than love?

She rubbed her chest and tried to shove back the fear and the tears. This needed to stop. She bit her lip.

Please let him be as good as Miranda said, as good as I think he is, because I need him to come home. To me.

Riya left the bathroom depleted. She found herself scratching her elbow and plucked the moisturizer off her nightstand as she tried to think of a distraction. The only solution was work. It had helped her out just a little bit the first four days that Gray had been on his mission. She walked past the destroyed bed, and went downstairs.

She snagged her bag pack and considered her computer tablet, but then pulled out the new composition notebook she'd begun writing in when she'd returned to San Diego. She fished out a pencil then went and sat cross-legged on the love seat. Einstein deigned to jump up and push up beside her and lick himself.

"Still worried about me, huh?" Einstein just blinked and yawned.

Riya opened up the notebook and looked over what she'd documented the last three days since she'd come home from Washington. She thought about the argument she'd had with the Lieutenant General in charge of the project at the Pentagon right before he'd ousted her from the project.

"I've never seen anything like this, Sir. Someone has developed an airborne contagion that has the ability to affect only the Y chromosome. Obviously they're intending to take it to the next logical stage."

Riya could see the steam pouring out of her temporary boss's ears. "English, explain this to me in English," he'd said.

"Think of the applications. They've figured out a way to isolate a poison so it just impacts a man, while totally bypassing a woman. I can only imagine they're going to try to pinpoint this down to other criteria like ethnicities, maybe even specific gene pools."

"Got it, men versus women," he'd glowered. "Are you trying to say they might be able to target actual families?"

"Yes! Can you imagine the application if it wasn't an airborne poison, but an actual treatment for a disease? I'm sure we could do things like target those people who were carriers of the sickle cell anemia gene. This is amazing work. I need to talk to the person who developed this."

The general crossed his arms. "That's not possible," he bit out.

She thrust her hands on her hips. "It has to be. The potential benefits are extraordinary. This is a critical breakthrough."

"You gave me the information I needed. It's time you went back to your lab in San Diego."

The next thing Riya knew, she was on a plane with all of her notes confiscated. Since she'd been working on a Pentagon computer and not allowed access to her personal computer, they'd figured she wouldn't be able to retain the information. Were they nuts? She had a photographic memory for God's sake. Couldn't the idiots read her file?

Riya prayed that at least part of her brain could focus on work, and not on Gray. She bent over her notebook and began sketching out the sequencing she'd witnessed from the pathogen. There had to be a way to reverse engineer it.

"DAMMIT!"

Her pencil careened across the page, scratching over her writing. Then a huge grin broke over her face as the second bong of Gray's distinctive text tone sounded. Riya untangled herself from the couch and made a mad dash upstairs to her phone.

Einstein yowled in protest and ran after her.

YOU UP?

Riya clutched her phone, and fumbled to answer Gray's text.

YES.

CAN I COME OVER?

Her hands were so slippery that she had to retype the word, YES.

BE THERE IN LESS THAN THIRTY.

Riya looked at the time on the phone. It was three-thirty in the morning. Miranda had said that Griff had often come back in the middle of the night. Did this mean that Gray wasn't even going home, he was coming straight to her?

She stumbled on the sheet that was hanging off the bed as she rushed to the bathroom. Einstein almost got caught under her feet.

"Any damage I do is going to be your fault," she warned. Pinning her braid on top of her head, she jumped in the shower and screeched under the cold water. She powered through until it warmed up. Nothing was going to stop her from getting ready.

When she got out of the shower she took a long time smoothing on her jasmine and raspberry lotion that she knew Gray liked. She frowned when she saw all the scratch marks. Now she didn't feel itchy at all.

You're a mess.

Just went to prove that a genius was as prone to psychosomatic responses as the next person.

She pulled out the lace lavender bra and panty set that she had purchased when she'd taken her sister out shopping. She'd been petting the satin and lace at least once a day since she'd brought them home, imagining Gray's reaction when he would see her in the lingerie. She shivered as she finally pulled it on.

She looked in her bedroom mirror and frowned when she noticed her hair. Riya yanked at the scrunchie holding her braid together, and dug her fingers through the long strands of her unwinding hair, trying to make it look nice.

Her doorbell rang.

For God's sake, it had barely been twenty minutes. To hell with her hair. Who cared what she was wearing. She whirled away from her mirror and stubbed her toe on her dresser as she raced to her bedroom door.

"Fuck!"

Oops, she was only wearing underwear. She grabbed her discarded sleepshirt and started tugging it over her head as she headed toward her stairs.

Stop.

Get a grip.

At the rate she was going she'd end up with a broken leg at the bottom of the stairs.

Riya untangled her right arm and got it into the sleeve of her pink shirt, and pulled it down so it covered her booty. Grabbing the handrail, she pounced down the stairs. She could do that, she was holding the rail after all.

Be smart.

Go home.

Go to bed.

Be smart.

He should never have texted Riya. What was he thinking? He was exhausted. He needed sleep. Desperately. But he needed to see Riya. He needed to touch her. Feel her warm and vibrant skin beneath his fingers, feel her warm breath against his lips. To see her eyes filled with light and laughter. It wasn't a want, it was a deep and compelling desire.

Gray relived those last few hours when he and his

men were in Bahrain. As soon as they crossed the border, they'd been met by members of the Fifth Fleet. He and his men had watched as Chantelle Briggs and Emily Hoag were taken from their care and put on a helicopter. Then Gray and the rest of his team went back to NSA Bahrain, and were separated. Gray went to go meet with the commanding officer, while his men went to go get something to eat.

Captain Reese was a smart man who had received the video from Dex showing Acting Commander Harry Morris in action. Reese was also wise enough to realize that it was more than likely someone connected with Black Dawn had arranged for Acting Commander Dumbass to have papers transferring him to Libya.

"Morris is on his way back here," Reese said with a steely glint in his eye. "I would have taken care of him on my own after receiving the video. I didn't appreciate you sending him around the world."

"Noted," Gray agreed. There was no way he was going to throw Wyatt under the bus for having done this. Actually it showed some initiative on the kid's part. But still Gray needed to teach him some discretion.

"Now that that's out of the way, I want to tell you I'm impressed with you and your team. You knocked it out of the park. But who are we kidding, that doesn't mean shit. You've impressed Baker, that's who really matters. Plus, your plan didn't kill him. Which I sincerely appreciate."

"How is he?" Gray asked. He'd only gotten the one report that the former SEAL was fine after the crash that had sent him over the bridge.

"He ended up with a couple of broken ribs. Of course he reported for duty the next day."

Any SEAL would have done the same thing.

"Any word on the women?" Gray asked.

"They were only airlifted to the hospital two hours ago, Lieutenant," Captain Reese sighed. "I asked my assistant to interrupt us with any news about their status. They were taken to the same hospital used by the Prince of Bahrain. It has the best facilities in the country."

"Are their families going to meet them?"

"Emily Hoag's mother is coming in from Oman, the Ambassador can't make it. It's my understanding that Ms. Brigg's estranged from most of her family, but a cousin is coming from Canada. The doctors have some concerns about both the women, for different reasons."

Gray knew exactly what he was talking about. "I want to be kept informed, even when I return to the states."

Reese gave him a considering look, then nodded. "You and your men did a damn good job. I hate the fact that one of mine got in our way."

Gray really didn't need to know why Harry Morris had been put in an acting commander position. It wasn't his business. But what *was* his business, is that he not be in a position to harm anyone in the future. He put men's lives at risk.

"Captain, with all due respect—" Gray began.

Reese cut him off. "I'm not going to go into a long drawn-out explanation," Reese said. "What I will tell you, is that Morris will never be in a position to put another man or team in harm's way. You have my word on that." Reese got up from behind his desk and held out his hand. Gray shook it.

"Your transport is already fueled up. Hopefully, we'll have an update on both women before you leave."

Gray caught up with his men as they were walking to the plane. Reese's sandy-haired assistant came running across the tarmac to talk to them.

"What's the news?" Gray demanded as all of his team gathered around the young man.

"Ms. Hoag isn't speaking to anyone. The doctors say that she'll be good to travel home to California in a couple of weeks with her mother."

"What about the Ambassador?" Griff crossed his arms staring down the smaller man.

The petty officer didn't flinch. "I was told that the Ambassador couldn't leave his post at this time, and it would just be Emily and her mother leaving to go stateside."

Gray could feel every one of his team making judgements about Emily's father, none of them good.

"I'm going to be keeping tabs on her," Dex said. "Just because she arrives back in the States, doesn't mean she's off our watch."

Gray's men nodded.

"And Chantelle Briggs?" Aiden asked. "How is she doing?"

"She's still in surgery." He pulled a piece of paper out of his pocket. "The doctor wanted me to tell you something verbatim. 'Whoever worked on Ms. Briggs in the field did an excellent job.'" The young man looked up and grinned.

"You still didn't answer my question," Aiden glared at him. "What kind of surgery is Chantelle having?"

"Oh, one of her broken ribs ended up perforating a lung, and they had to go in and repair that. They don't expect any problems." Gray watched as Aiden relaxed the slightest little bit.

Dex turned to Aiden. "Don't worry, man. Wyatt and I will be keeping tabs on Ms. Briggs as well."

"Your ass would have been in a sling if you hadn't," Aiden glowered.

"Okay men, get moving," Gray waved to the plane. "The sooner we board, the sooner we're home."

That was the only good news that the members of Black Dawn had before they loaded up on the plane. For the first half hour of the trip home, Gray replayed the mission, beating himself up. Was there any way that they could have gotten to the women when they were still at the resort? If they had, could they have saved Emily from the atrocities visited on her by Faizon and his son?

He allowed himself exactly thirty minutes of worthless thinking before shutting that shit down. He and his team would do a post-mortem of the mission when they got home, they would determine what went right and what went wrong. But analytically, Gray knew that with Harry Morris in their way, they got to Saudi Arabia as quickly as they could. Aiden and Dex had worked wonders figuring out the Golden Tulip, and they'd had no choice but to wait until the middle of the night to raid the boat.

It was a subdued group that landed in San Diego. Wyatt wasn't at the base, and all the men left to go home to their women. Gray had intended to go home, there was no way he was planning on subjecting his dark mood on Riya. But here he was at her door, waiting for her to open it.

He heard the click of the alarm being unarmed, and then she unbolted the door, and there she was. He could breathe again.

"Gray?"

He realized he had been standing there without speaking.

"I've missed you." His voice was rough.

She grasped his hand and tugged. "Come in."

9

GRAY WAS A SIGHT FOR SORE EYES. THE BLACK T-SHIRT HE wore molded to his upper body, and made her ache, but when she looked into his face all of her naughty thoughts flew out the window. The man looked exhausted. More than that, he looked ravaged.

Riya put her hand over his heart. "Gray, what happened?"

He shook his head, as if coming out of a dream, then smiled down at her. "You're beautiful."

Had she dreamed that expression on his face? No. She hadn't.

"Talk to me. Are you okay?"

"I'm fine. A little tired. Hungry. Happy to see you." He cupped her cheek, his thumb doing that thing he did, caressing her lower lip, causing shivers to race through every cell of her body.

"Is everybody else okay? Griff?"

"Everybody's fine. I promise."

"Let's get you something to eat."

"You're kidding, right? Food can wait. It's you I want. You I need."

The heat in his eyes could melt steel. Riya trembled, and Gray wrapped his arms around her. Was he holding her up, or did he just want her close? Did it matter as long as she was pressed up against him?

Riya sank her nails into his shoulders, trying to force him to lower his head. Then he did.

Gray's mouth touched hers and she thrilled at the sensations that ran up and down her spine. He brushed his lips back and forth against hers, until he coaxed her to open with a sigh of contentment. Like the marauder he was, he took advantage and stroked his tongue inside her mouth and gathered her closer, when her knees weakened.

She needed.

She wanted.

She sucked him deeper inside, sliding her tongue against his, exalting in every single one of the new sensations that Gray provided.

He tangled his hand in her hair and pulled at it. The tugs in counterpoint with the thrusts of his tongue. She was going to explode.

What was that noise?

Was it a whimper? A moan?

Gray reared back and gave her a penetrating look. "Baby, are you okay?"

"What?" She didn't understand. "Why did you stop?"

His shoulder relaxed just the tiniest little bit beneath her hand. She moved it to stroke his whiskers.

"I was worried, the noise you made, it sounded like I might have hurt you."

"Oh, I was the one I heard," she grimaced. "Gray, you've never, ever hurt me." She cuddled up closer to him. "Being close to you feels wonderful."

He let out a sigh of relief. As much as she wanted to continue the kissing portion of the evening, it seemed that Gray was a little too tightly wound for that. She gave him another hug, willing him to relax. It took a solid two minutes before she felt the tension drain out of him.

"Now are you ready for some food?" she asked as she pulled back to look him in the face.

His eyes lit up. "What do you have?"

"Tandoori chicken and rice or Hawaiian pizza."

It was fun to see Gray shudder in distaste.

"Pineapple on pizza is an offense to all that is holy."

"Tandoori chicken it is, unless you want me to make you a grilled cheese sandwich and warm up some tomato soup."

"Are you kidding? I want the chicken. All I've had is an MRE since yesterday."

He started to follow her into the kitchen.

"Sit down, Big Guy. I'm bringing it out to you." She shoved him toward the couch, but he didn't budge.

"I really want to go into the kitchen with you." His voice was rough, in a sexy sort of way.

"Why?"

"I can't wait to see you bend down to pull things out of the refrigerator."

Holy hell!

Riya looked down. How had she not remembered she was only wearing her sleep shirt?

"Let me go upstairs. I'll be right back."

Gray grabbed her hand before she could make a run for it.

"Are you cold?"

He had often teased her about keeping the temperature up above seventy degrees at all times. So he knew she wasn't. She shook her head.

"Don't feel like you have to get dressed up for me. Anyway, besides getting a chance to see your sexy legs, your shirt is cracking me up."

She looked down at the phrase adorning her chest, and giggled.

"You like that, do you?"

"I met a man while I was overseas, who wouldn't catch the joke."

"You've got to be kidding."

She plucked at her shirt so she could get a better look at the saying.

Five out of four people struggle with math.

"Uhm, Riya, I can almost see your panties when you do that." Gray's voice was strangled.

She blushed from the tip of her toes to her forehead. "I'll go change," she whispered.

"Don't you dare. I'm serious, I want to ogle you in your kitchen."

She felt that rumbly voice all the way to her toes. She could always stoop to pull things out of her fridge, instead of bending.

Gray yawned, and all thought of stooping and bending fled her mind. "You are relegated to the couch.

I'm warming up some food for you. If you last long enough tonight, I'll give you a small peek at the color of underwear I'm wearing, but only if you're a good boy."

What the hell, it was what she'd been hoping to do anyway. But more important than anything else, was taking care of Gray. He looked dead on his feet, he needed to eat and rest. As she saw him sink down into the cushions, she wondered if he would even be awake when she brought out the food.

"Gray?"

Gray recognized the pearl gray glow of dawn lighting the room. Riya's face came into view.

"You look uncomfortable as all get out. I hate sleeping on this couch, and I'm half your size."

Gray stretched his neck and winced, then he laughed. "This is a dream bed compared to a lot of places I've slept."

"Come upstairs, and you can have a real bed. Or I can make you breakfast before you go to bed."

"That sounds like heaven."

Gray swung his legs over the side of the couch and planted his feet onto the carpet. He vaguely remembered taking his boots off.

"What sounds like heaven?" Riya asked.

Gray grinned up at her. "Either. Both." He took a look at Riya and was disappointed to see she was now wearing jeans and a sweater.

"Well that's as clear as mud," she smiled.

Gray itched to pull Riya into his arms, but he ran

his tongue over his teeth. He'd taken a shower, brushed his teeth and put on clean clothes at the base in Coronado before heading to Riya's. But now that his teeth had grown hair, he'd kill to grab his toothbrush from the duffel in his car.

"First, I need to go grab some stuff out of my car and head to the bathroom."

He looked over to his right and saw that his boots weren't standing neatly at the end of the couch, which was odd. They were on their side, and one of them was being pulled, ever so slowly, under the couch by the shoelace. He could make out Einstein's blue eyes glinting from under the sofa.

It all made sense now.

"I'll have waffles ready by the time you're done."

"Orange juice?" he asked hopefully.

"Bacon too," she promised.

Gray tugged his footwear from a disappointed cat and got off the couch and went to the front door. When he put his hand on the doorknob, he frowned.

"Riya," he called out.

She poked her head around to the end of the hall. "Yes?"

"You didn't set the alarm."

He watched her brow furrow. "Darn it. That's the first time since you installed it that I've forgotten. I had it set last night before you came over. I think your arrival just took me by surprise."

"This is important," he cautioned.

"Gray, I'm not being flighty about this. If you thought it was essential that it be installed, of course

I'm going to use it. You showing up at three in the morning made me forget. I'm sorry."

He looked at her and saw that she was sincere, and soon to be sincerely pissed if he continued to make a big deal out of it.

"No need to be sorry, Honey. Your safety is important to me, that's all."

Her expression smoothed out into a smile. "I know it is, Gray. If I didn't realize you were coming from a place of caring, I would have booted you and your friends out on your collective asses when you came over to install the damn thing."

She would have, too.

Gray grinned as he walked out into the cool, early morning air. He grabbed the duffel out of the backseat of his SUV. It was Friday morning and he didn't need to be back to base until Monday. He was going to do his best to see if he could talk Riya into playing hooky with him today.

She heard the shower turn off upstairs, which was her cue to pour the second round of batter into the waffle iron, turn on the burner underneath the bacon and start beating the eggs. The coffee was already brewing. Riya was going to be sad to see all that delicious blond scruff shaved away. It hadn't developed into a full-blown beard, it was just that right amount of whiskers that made him look oh-so-sexy.

"Smells good in here."

Egg mix went flying out of the bowl as she whirled

around to see Gray standing in low-slung jeans and a white t-shirt.

"Didn't mean to startle you." He grabbed a paper towel and wiped up the egg that had spilled while she just ogled him. In the bright morning light she could see the white interspersed with the blond in his whiskers.

How gorgeous was that?

Pull it together.

She sidestepped him and snagged a glass from the cupboard and poured him a big glass of orange juice, then gave a chin tilt toward one of the stools at the kitchen bar. "Do you want to just eat here? Or in the dining room?"

"Here's great. But, why don't I help you?" He sipped from his glass and his left hand swept down her back. She'd forgotten Gray's habit of casual touching.

"The kitchen is too small for the two of us. You sit there and talk to me."

Riya knew it was because he'd been on a mission. He couldn't tell her anything. Same went for her, she couldn't tell him that she'd been to DC, and she sure as hell couldn't tell him that she'd been trying to recreate things from memory. He must have seen her hesitation.

"I've got a better idea, you talk to me. I want to hear about microbes, microcosms, and Microsoft," Gray said with an easy smile.

"Microsoft stock is up, even though there is a bug in their latest Windows release. I'm going to leave the microcosms to the ecologists, and which microbes do you want to talk about? Bacteria? Eukaryotes? Protists?"

"I give, I give?" The man's laugh was a thing of

beauty. "Tell me gossip. Or tell me if you've babysat. Tell me if you visited your parents or your sisters. What's the latest with Anika?"

Riya flushed with pleasure as she plated the two waffles, mounds of eggs and six slices of bacon and put it in front of Gray. He always remembered what was going on in her life. She would bet her bottom dollar that he'd done some reading up on molecular virology the same as she had on Navy SEALs, and he might even know a little bit about Eukaryotes if push came to shove. The man was crazy smart when he studied up on something.

She noticed he hadn't picked up his fork. "Come on, dig in."

"I'll wait for you."

"It'll get cold. I have to wait for the next waffle to come out."

He just lifted his eyebrow and she turned back to the counter, willing her waffle to hurry up and cook.

Damn Southern manners.

She grabbed her food when the timer went off, and sat across from him. Their eyes locked, forks forgotten.

Gray reached out and tugged her hand across the smooth bar top. "I missed you." They were the same words he'd said last night. He'd even used the same rough voice.

Riya blinked back tears.

"I was scared," she admitted softly. "I tried real hard not to be. I concentrated on the Microsoft stock, but it didn't do it for me." Her laughter was forced. "Can you tell me anything?"

"I can tell you that I work with the best team in the

world, and that they've never let me down." His eyes roamed over her face, then flicked down to her plate for just an instant.

She pulled back her hand. "Eat. Then we can talk. You can tell me the stuff that isn't confidential. Then I'll return the favor and tell you about *my* stuff that isn't classified."

Gray grabbed the butter dish and slathered half a stick onto his two waffles, then proceeded to drown them in syrup. He laughed at her expression. "One of the things I can tell you, is that there weren't a lot of carbs, fats or sugars where I was. I'm making up for it."

Riya ate some of her food, then got up and put another serving of batter into the waffle iron.

"You're a goddess," Gray said looking up from his empty plate. She brought the bottle of orange juice to the countertop and filled up Gray's glass then snuck one of her slices of bacon onto his plate.

"I'm not taking your food. Anyway, I'm still not done with my bacon."

"I'm done. If I wanted it, I'd eat it."

Gray eyed her carefully, then grinned. He broke it in half. He popped one half into his mouth, the other he dropped onto the floor for Einstein.

"Gray, he's going to be begging at the table for weeks now," Riya complained.

He didn't look guilty in the slightest. Einstein was already finished with the bacon and was looking up at her expectantly.

"No," she said to him.

He gave her a snooty meow, then stalked out of the kitchen.

Gray burst out laughing.

While he was laughing, Riya pulled the next waffle out of the iron, and put it on his plate. This time he didn't use as much butter or syrup.

"Cutting back?"

"I have my eye on tasting something sweeter after breakfast." The look in his eyes, and the rumble in his voice left her in no doubt as to what he was talking about. "Riya, stop staring and tell me some stories, otherwise we're heading to bed."

"Aren't you," she started, then gulped. "Don't you?" Dammit, her voice squeaked. "Aren't you tired?"

"Not when I'm looking at you."

Riya damn near knocked over her glass of orange juice as she reached for it. Her mouth had never been this dry.

"Stories Riya, I need stories." He took a leisurely bite of waffle, his eyes drifting down her torso, settling on her breasts. She gulped down more juice. Stories. She could talk. She knew she could.

"My sister Anika came over. I was proud of her for leaving her boys with Mom. I thought Dev might have to be surgically removed from her hip. She and I went clothes shopping."

"Anika?" Gray's eyes darted upwards in surprise.

"I know, right? She didn't do anything drastic like try on jeans. But she did try on a pair of tailored slacks."

"But she just ended up with dresses," Gray guessed.

"You got it right. However, one of them showed her knees. I almost fell over in a dead faint. Maryam told me that there is a man at the community center who has been asking Anika out. Gray, she's been divorced for three years now, so I think my sister might actually go for it. We're all praying for her."

"From everything you've told me, she deserves happiness."

What a sweet thing for him to say.

Riya looked down at Gray's empty plate. She took a deep breath. "Let me show you where you can sleep." As she walked around the counter, Gray's arm reached out and wrapped around her waist and he tugged her toward him.

"Come here."

She fell against his body, her hands landing on his muscled chest.

"If I moan, will you know it's with pleasure?"

His eyes twinkled. "Now that you've warned me, I will."

"Uhm," her voice trailed off. What was she going to say? She was going to say something, wasn't she?

Gray pushed back a lock of her hair, and ever so slowly pushed it behind her ear. Weeks ago he'd realized that she was sensitive there, and he used that knowledge now, gently tracing his fingers along her delicate skin. Riya sucked in air.

"That's not a moan," he whispered warmly against her ear.

Oh God, the feel of his breath made her heart speed up and her head fall back.

Would he?

She gasped as his teeth closed down softly on her lobe, then his tongue licked. She needed to do something, but the world was getting fuzzy.

Think.

Don't just feel.

Think.

Her hands drifted downwards, savoring the heat and hardness of his toned torso. She yanked at the soft cotton of his shirt, and shoved her hand underneath so that she could touch the warm, muscled flesh. Her hands pushed against him, enjoying the feel of her man. She pushed higher, until her fingers threaded through the hair on his chest and found his heartbeat.

So caught up in the beauty of Gray's body, Riya shuddered as she felt long fingers stroking beneath the waistband of her jeans. When had he unbuttoned her? When she felt his calloused palm skim under her panties and cup her butt, all questions flew out of her mind, all that mattered was his touch setting her on fire.

"We have a moan." His voice was hoarse. "That means pleasure, right?"

"That means bedtime," she corrected.

"Thank God. I'm sick of your couch."

Her fingers pressed into his chest as he swept her up into his arms.

"Don't you dare try to carry me up those stairs. They're too narrow." Riya tried to wiggle out of his hold.

Gray looked down at her and laughed. "Dr. Patel, if you don't behave, you'll find yourself over my shoulder."

"You wouldn't."

The gleam in his eyes said he would. She stopped moving.

When he got to the top of the stairs he went directly

to her room. How did he know which one was hers? Then she remembered he'd showered up here. He'd done that damned reconnaissance thing again.

"Pulling up the comforter over a messy bed is not the same thing as making your bed, you know that don't you?" Gray asked as he pulled down the comforter and the blanket and sheet and settled her on the bed.

Riya shot back up and off the bed.

"What are you doing? I liked you where you were."

"I have to get naked, don't I?" She pulled her sweater over her head and folded it up. She put it on the chair beside the bed. When she turned around, she saw Gray just standing there. Hesitantly, she started to undo the front of her bra. He walked over and stilled her hands.

"Can we slow down just a little bit?"

What the hell? Did I read this wrong, too?

He'd carried her up the stairs for God's sake. She looked down at the front of his jeans. Yep, still interested.

"I don't understand." She tried to stop her voice from quivering.

"I kind of get that. It's just that I like unwrapping my own gifts. And the first time I get to make love to you is a gift I will treasure for the rest of my life."

Riya bent her head just a bit then looked up at him through her bangs. She didn't want him to be able to see her eyes in case he was teasing. He couldn't really mean that could he? But please say he did.

Please.

"Riya?" His voice stroked softly across her heart.

She'd never seen anything shine like the brilliant sincerity in his eyes. This man meant every word. He was honor. He was beauty. He was truth.

"Nothing in my life has ever felt this right," she whispered.

10

Her words pierced his soul.

He grasped her wrist and kissed her fingertips. "Ahhhh Riya, you mean the world to me."

He could drown in the mystery of her black eyes. He kissed her. How could he not? The feel of her lips against his, so plush, so soft, felt like heaven. He slowly turned her so that he could lower her onto the bed, her arms falling above her head. He loved watching her mass of dark hair contrasting against her lavender sheets.

She was beautiful. Gray trailed his knuckles from her fingertips to the insides of her elbows, watching her undulate as he continued downwards. Inwards. Until his fingers drifted softly over the mounds of her generous breasts to the clasp, and then he slowly unfastened her bra. He moved the lacy cups aside so that he could touch her pretty brown nipples. They peaked as he caressed them.

"You're so soft and sensitive." His finger traced

around and around. Gray smiled tightly as he watched her shudder.

"Please," she begged.

It was his pleasure. Her breast was supple and firm, he ached as he caressed her. He thumbed one nipple as he bent his head and lashed the other with his tongue. He'd imagined raspberries, but this was so much better, it was the taste of Riya. He needed more.

He lifted her up, as he continued to torture them both. Soon her bra was gone, then he had her jeans off and was tracing the front of her silk panties when she grabbed his ears.

"Do I get to unwrap my package?" Her voice was sultry.

"Honey, holding my ears is not the way to get me out of my clothes," he pointed out.

In a flash, her hands moved, and she was grabbing the neck of his t-shirt and pulling it over his head. Gray helped. He liked her purr of satisfaction, but he liked the feel of his skin against her skin even better. She did a slow slide along his chest, her nipples rasping against his flesh.

"My God, Woman, you're going to be the death of me."

"I can't help it. I need this. I need you."

He heard the chaotic tremor in her voice. He kissed the side of her mouth, she turned her head and captured his lips in a frantic kiss. Gray slid his hand down the front of her panties and found her swollen flesh. Riya arched up with a cry of need. He had a moment of primal satisfaction go through him as he realized how caught up Riya was in their intimacy. He had never had a woman who so equally matched his passion.

Gray parted her wet folds and relished the sounds of satisfaction that she made. He circled the nub of her clitoris and she began to shake, then she thrashed her head to the side. He pinched, and she buried her teeth in his shoulder, muffling her shriek.

As she came off her high, she laved the bite marks she had made with her talented tongue.

He levered off the bed, trying to remember where he'd left his duffle bag.

He needed the goddamn condoms.

Now!

Gray pulled out the foil package and turned to see Riya looking at him with glittering eyes. One leg was crooked up. He yanked off his belt and had his jeans stripped off by the time he was back at the bed.

"You weren't wearing underwear." She sounded kind of taken aback as he pulled off her panties and spread her legs so he could stare at her. "Why weren't you—"

As he thought, when he took that first subtle taste of her exquisite flesh she stopped asking inane questions. It was a good thing, because all he was capable of was relishing Riya and praying he would be able to muster enough control so that he could give her an orgasm when he entered her. Gray caressed her silky thighs and held them open as he lavished attention on her swollen flesh. He was drunk from the essence of Riya.

Once again he felt those tell-tale shimmers start

vibrating through her body. He pushed up so he could see her face as she gasped in pleasure.

"You're beautiful. I could spend a lifetime watching you like this."

She mewled in protest. Gray stood, and sheathed himself. He stroked his hand down the outside of her thigh. Such soft skin.

"Don't tease."

"I'm not, Honey."

She reached out with her hand. "Come closer."

He put one knee down on the bed, and positioned his cock at her entrance. He couldn't wait a moment longer. He pressed in slowly, and felt her welcoming warmth.

"So good," she sighed on a long breath.

Gray couldn't even get words out to agree. He pushed in further, incredulous that the sensations kept getting better and better as she tightened around him. He eased himself down so that he rested some of his weight on top of her, her soft skin a delight against his.

Her smile was tremulous, so he pushed the hair off her face so that he could clearly see her eyes. They held so much emotion. It was as if his heart were reflected there. His gaze roamed along the beautiful lines of her elegant jaw to the rapid beat of her pulse. He peppered kisses down her neck toward her breast, as he began to move inside her.

Riya's sighs shot through him, like lightening in a desert sky. When her nails sank into his back, he sucked her nipple deep into his mouth, gorging himself on her flavor, on her uninhibited responses.

She scored her fingers down his flesh until she

gripped his ass, her heels dug into his thighs and she undulated upwards, her efforts eager and a little uncoordinated.

"Help me," she begged.

Gray changed tactics, and gently licked her delicate skin, continuing his smooth thrusts even though her body tempted him beyond bearing.

"We have all the time in the world," he soothed.

"We do?"

He moved his hand and trailed it along her side, down past her waist, to her hip. He curved around and clutched her smooth flank, sinking deep and finding that perfect spot that had her head arching back in the pillow.

"Gray," she cried. Her head thrashed.

"I have you."

He'd lied, he couldn't wait.

Her body was music that he couldn't resist. He needed her, and he had to make this perfect for her.

Some part of him noted the sting of her nails, but it was just one more layer of sensation that flavored his pleasure. He clenched his jaw and stared at Riya, taking note of her desperation. He smiled, knowing what was coming.

"Look at me," he commanded.

He waited until her beautiful onyx eyes were fixed on his and then gave that final thrust. He saw that dawning look of comprehension as she cried out her release.

Thank you, God.

Pleasure so acute that it was pain gathered at the base of his spine, as he took flight, and his woman watched him. Her joy in his ecstasy was incandescent, and he felt her body shudder in bliss again.

It took them a matter of seconds to find just the right position to get comfortable for a morning nap. It would have been faster, if they didn't have to accommodate a needy Siamese.

BEAUTIFUL BLUE EYES. But they weren't all soft and romantic anymore. What was going on? Riya pulled the sheet up around herself and sat up in bed. The sun streamed brightly through the slats of her bedroom blinds and Gray was looking all SEAL-y.

"What's wrong? You're the one who came in last, if the alarm wasn't set, it's on you, Tyler," she defended herself in a teasing voice.

Gray didn't say anything, and she realized his eyes were almost gray, like his name. Like they were filled with storm clouds.

"Gray?"

Slowly she scooched up against the headboard.

He caught her hand in his then pulled her arm straight and turned it over. His voice was tight as he asked. "What in the hell happened to your arms? It's the same on both sides. Who scratched you so badly?"

"I'm fine," she rushed to reassure him.

"Who?" His voice was sharp.

"Gray, nobody did anything to me. I did this to myself. I was itchy. I scratched."

"You scratched yourself raw? You broke the skin?" Gray clearly didn't believe her. "Tell me what really happened, Honey." His voice alarmed her, but his touch was exquisitely tender as he traced her damaged flesh. With her free hand, she pulled the sheet up higher up her chest, Gray saw her movement.

"Don't hide yourself from me. Are there other marks? How did I miss them earlier?"

"Calm down. That's the worst of it."

"The worst?" His voice rose with the question. He tugged at the sheet, and his gaze swept over her body. "Where, where else?"

She drew the sheet down farther, so he could see the tops of her knees. "Here. I don't know why it flared on my joints." She then pointed to her ankle. "I'm such an idiot."

"What are you talking about? These really do look like you might have scratched here. These look like the size of your nails." He traced the welts on her left knee that showed clearly in the afternoon sun.

"I told you I did it, why would I lie?" Riya pulled up the sheet again. Before she could put her arms under the cloth, he took her arm.

"This looks bad. Was it an allergic reaction? Did you see a doctor?" He closely examined the worst scratches where she had drawn blood. He looked pale. "You really hurt yourself, Riya."

"You don't see a doctor for a psychosomatic problem. It was all in my mind, and I'm not even itchy anymore."

His eyes shot to hers. "Explain."

How embarrassing.

"It's not a big deal, and it's stopped." She leaned sideways to grab the bottle of moisturizer off the nightstand. "I just needed this." She bent her head and mumbled. "And you home."

"What did you say?"

She didn't answer.

"What do you mean psychosomatic? Talk to me."

"Can we have this talk after I've put on my clothes?"

She pulled at the sheet, and he caught her. "Stop just a minute, will you? I need to understand what's going on."

His voice sounded funny so she looked up at him. He looked really confused, like he couldn't comprehend what she was saying. Her shoulders sagged. She didn't want to have to be more specific, because then he would have to admit what a fool she'd been.

"Gray, seriously, it's nothing," she choked out.

His expression grew dark and he shoved back the covers. "Fine." He stalked to the bathroom and came back moments later with her first aid kit.

"You're making too big of a deal about this."

He sat down beside her and tugged on her arm, and examined her elbow. "No I'm not, this could get infected. Especially when you're cleaning the cat box. You need to have this covered up."

The atmosphere was tense while he took his time smoothing antibiotic cream on her wounds. She hated it.

"Now, will you tell me why you were scratching." He asked evenly. She looked at his face and tried to read his expression, but he was avoiding her. Gray didn't do that. He was always careful to meet her eyes, it was like he understood she needed to see his expression clearly to understand where he was coming from.

"Will you please look at me?" He continued to minister to her. His concentration intensely focused on her arm. When she hissed in a breath, his gaze shot up and met hers. He looked anguished.

"My God, Gray. What's wrong?" How could he be so upset? It made no sense. It was only a scratch.

He didn't respond, he just stared at her, and she saw such hell roiling around in his eyes.

"Gray, talk to me."

"I just hate seeing you in pain, it tears me up inside." Riya had to strain to hear him.

Her mind started going through all of the moments she had been with him like a fast rolodex, until she stopped on that moment in front of the church when she'd slipped. Yeah, he'd been concerned, but it wasn't this level of distress. This was over the top, and it had to be in reaction to something that had happened recently. Was it because they'd just made love? Was he regretting it? That didn't make sense in the slightest. He was obsessed that she was injured? Why all of a sudden? It was totally out of proportion to the situation? What had...?

"Gray, was a woman hurt on your mission?"

His eyes widened.

She lifted her hand. "I don't want any details. I'm not trying to pry, I know that's not how we can operate if we're going to be a couple. But I needed to understand why you were acting like you were."

Gray ripped open the bandage and tenderly applied it to her skin, then heaved off of the bed. "I'm reacting the way I am because I don't want the woman I care for to be injured, or in pain, or to risk further damage on my watch."

Riya saw the way he was clenching his fist. He stalked over to her dresser, Einstein had to run to avoid being trampled. Gray was oblivious. That meant he was really upset. She took a deep breath. Somehow she needed to fix this. She fought back her panic.

Think.

She took a deep breath.

Truth.

She needed to come clean.

"I was sad," she blurted out.

Gray tilted his head. "Huh?"

"I was sad because I was missing you. I was worried about you being on a mission. I didn't figure it all out until today that that was the reason I was so itchy. Gray, it wasn't a big deal. It was all in my head. Sad and worried makes me scratch myself."

He went stock still.

His voice was a low rumble. "So I was the one who caused this? It was because of me?"

Oh, shit.

He sounded like a wounded animal.

"No, of course it's not your fault," she cried. "It was all me."

He marched over and rested his fists on either side of her hips. "Don't lie. Don't sugar-coat this, Riya. You were hurting so badly, that you tore at your skin until you bled!"

Her hands shot up and cupped his cheeks, she

barely noticed the sheet slipping down her body. "This is not your fucking issue."

"Bullshit." His breath was hot.

She could feel tears building. This was big. This was monumental. She needed to diffuse this. He needed to think, not feel.

"Do I look like her?" she asked calmly.

She could see Gray's immediate understanding. "No, you look nothing like her," he answered slowly.

She didn't say anything, just let him gnaw on that for long moments. She noted that his shoulders relaxed the tiniest little bit.

"But Riya, ultimately it was because you worried about me that caused you to hurt yourself."

She nodded. "But I finally figured it out. I'll get it under control. It was a gut reaction because I care so deeply." She gave him a small smile. "Ring a bell?"

He sat back on his haunches. "Maybe."

She stifled a giggle.

"Are you going to laugh at me? Because I might have to retaliate."

She sighed in relief. Crisis diverted.

Riya lunged at Gray. "I need a hug."

Aw, hell.

Where were the tears coming from? He was going to go SEAL-y again.

"Don't you dare go crazy again, these are tears of relief. You scared me."

He stroked her back.

She felt a shudder go through his big body.

"I reserve the right to care too much in the future," he whispered.

She hiccupped, trying to stem her tears.

"Like now. Just let it out, Baby, I'm home now. The only scratching is on my back, got it?"

She snorted.

"Got it."

11

"HEY, THE RUBBER BAND CAR JUST PULLED UP," WYATT yelled out across Aiden and Evie O'Malley's backyard. He was in a position to see their driveway from the corner where he was sitting to rest his leg.

Dammit, Gray had known the guys were going to give her shit for her car.

Miranda Porter stalked over to Wyatt from where she had been standing on the patio with the other women. She glowered down at the sandy haired SEAL who put his arms up over his head in mock defense.

"Leeds, if you do anything to make my friend feel bad, I will pluck out your nipple hairs. You get me?" Miranda's steely words could be heard across the lawn.

All talking stopped as a collective wince went through the crowd. Gray chuckled when he saw two of his teammates cross their arms over their chests.

Griff sauntered over from the grill, with his daughter on his hip. "Honey, Wyatt didn't mean anything by it. He's just teasing about Riya's Prius," Griff tried to soothe his wife.

"Well, he better cool it." She plucked little Livvie out of her husband's arms and went back to join the women.

Evie O'Malley came up next to Gray. "Are you going to introduce me to your Riya? I've been dying to meet her." The petite brunette locked her arm through his and led him through the screen door to the front of the house.

The doorbell rang just as they reached it. Evie opened it and grinned.

"Hello," she greeted Riya.

Gray saw Riya's tentative smile. Then she pushed out a huge store-bought tray of brownies.

"I'm in love with you," Evie clapped her hands. "You brought my kryptonite."

"You like chocolate, too?" Riya asked hopefully.

"I *love* chocolate, especially brownies. Did Miranda tell you?" Evie took the tray. "Come in."

Gray was about to introduce them, but Evie, in her typical style, started talking.

"Oh fuck, I'm Evie. I know you're Riya. Miranda told me how beautiful you are. I couldn't miss the long black hair. I always wanted straight hair instead of curls. Come into the kitchen. I'm going to break into these babies right now with a big ole glass of milk. Want me to set you up with the same?"

Riya looked up at him with a look of almost panic as Evie sped ahead.

"It's okay, she's always like this with everyone."

"Really?"

"Really." He looked her up and down. "You look gorgeous."

Riya's panicked look turned into a frown. "I'm wearing a university sweatshirt. Are you going to say I look gorgeous no matter what I wear?"

"More than likely, because you're a beautiful woman. Piper is going to UCSD so you're going to have a sure-fire friend."

"How many people are here? I thought you said it was a small barbeque."

"Probably thirty people." He saw her take a deep breath. He slid his hand under her hair and started to knead the tight tendons in her neck. "It's going to be fine. Just pretend they're the Pentagon types, you deal with them all the time."

"Yeah, but that's when it's in my field of expertise. These are your friends."

"You'll do great. Miranda and I have been bragging about you, so you're golden."

"Great," she muttered.

Gray laughed. He wrapped his arm around her and guided her to the kitchen. He wasn't surprised to see that Evie had two plates with brownies on them along with two glasses of milk at the kitchen table.

"This looks wonderful," Riya said with a genuine smile. "I've been at the lab since five this morning. I was hoping to have one of these to make up for my lack of breakfast and lunch."

While Evie's back was turned, Gray leaned over to whisper in Riya's ear. "You skipped breakfast and lunch?"

"I got caught up on a side project, and I had to make up time on my actual work."

Evie turned around in time to catch what Riya was saying.

"I hope you're not letting him ride roughshod. I have a husband and a brother who think they rule the world. They don't. Let's eat these brownies, and then you can join the ladies on the patio. We'll tell you how to handle these alpha males," Evie said with her Southern accent.

Gray enjoyed watching Riya carefully consider Evie's invitation and then see her eyes light up. He knew she only knew Miranda, and without Susan here as a buffer, this was big.

"I'll definitely join you after the brownies." She gave Gray a teasing look.

"You are not just having sugar to make up for two missed meals, Dr. Patel," Gray admonished.

Two sets of black eyes rolled at him. He laughed.

"Chocolate makes the world go round." Evie said sanctimoniously.

"Aiden would take my side." Gray shook his head at the two women, then watched as Riya took a large bite of her brownie.

RIYA LIKED EVIE A LOT, and not just because she was pint-sized like she was.

"Your house is beautiful," she complimented from her seat at the table.

"It was all Aiden. He had it before he married me. The man has taste."

"And that's why he married you." Marrying Evie was the best thing that ever happened to Aiden,at least that's what Gray had told Riya. Looking at their lovely house and Evie's obvious happiness, she confirmed it herself.

Evie moaned as she bit into her brownie. Then she took a deep swig of her milk. She set it down, then put her elbow on the table and stared at Riya. "I'm so impressed you're a scientist. That is so fucking cool. What made you decide to do that? What kind of science do you study?"

Over Evie's head, Riya watched as Gray casually opened up the refrigerator and started pulling out cold cuts and salads.

"One of my doctorates is in molecular virology. I want to cure diseases."

Riya was horrified as Evie's eyes started to water. She grabbed Riya's hand. "That is so noble."

"Wait a minute," Riya ripped her hand away and held it up. "It's also because it was the thing I was good at. I'm not noble or special or anything."

"Sure you are. You're trying to help people. You're trying to make the world better. You're not a taker. You're not a user. You're one of the good guys."

This woman was fierce.

Riya almost jumped out of her skin when she felt Gray's hand rest on her shoulder. She looked up at him helplessly.

"Evie is one of the good guys, too. She's a hero."

Riya watched as the little woman blushed.

Gray set down a plate that held some rolled up turkey slices, cheese squares, coleslaw and a dab of potato salad. It was exactly what she would have chosen. She picked up a cheese square.

"Are you talking about my sister, the heroine?" Riya jumped and dropped the piece of cheese onto her plate at the deep roar that filled the room. She heard a child chortle, which was the only reason she wasn't looking for a hiding place.

"Hello, Drake," Gray said to a man who was even bigger than he was. Riya stared at him for a long moment. He looked familiar. Then she realized he had the same genetics as the woman sitting across from her. *Oh yeah, he'd said sister.* If he hadn't been carrying a child, he would have truly scared her.

"Give me Andrew." Evie jumped out of her chair and made a grab for the toddler who was trying to wiggle out of the man's hold.

"Gray, we're all waiting to meet Riya," Drake said.

The big man turned to her and gave her a bright smile. "My name's Drake Avery. Only believe half of what people tell you about me. Unless it's my wife. Then you can believe everything. She loves me. She'll say good things."

Riya watched as Evie stepped out of the house with the little boy. Drake walked over to the counter and grabbed one of the brownies off the tray. She watched in amazement as he ate it in three big bites. "Heaven," he sighed.

Gray seemed to know how overwhelming Drake was because he stayed at her side. "Eat," he whispered. She picked up the piece of cheese and took a tiny bite.

"I hear you took a man out in one fell swoop with your stun-gun. Good going. You could be one of my sisters," Drake grinned at her. He poured himself a glass of milk. "Gray, you want one?"

"I'm going to grab a beer when dinner's up."

Drake came over and sat in the seat Evie had vacated, then he frowned at her plate. "Why do you have a plate of food? Dinner should be up in a half-hour."

"She didn't eat breakfast or lunch," Gray explained.

Drake scowled. "Well, that's stupid. Aren't you a doctor? You should know better. Eat."

Riya's stomach clenched and she set down the cheese. The man was overwhelming.

"Avery, back off," Gray commanded. He sounded pissed.

Drake looked over her shoulder at Gray, clearly confused. "I'm just trying to help."

"Your kind of help, we don't need."

"I need to go to the bathroom," Riya said, pushing away from the table. It was a lie, but she needed to get out of there...now.

"Let me show you where it is," Drake stood up.

"You've done enough. I'll show her." Gray touched her elbow and gave her an encouraging smile.

"You can just point, I really don't need a guide."

He pointed to a hallway. "First door on the right."

Riya made a quick escape. She sighed as soon as she made it inside.

Talk about testosterone poisoning. She ran cold water over her wrists, then used the toilet. She took a few more moments to calm herself. When she left the bathroom, it was just Gray waiting at the table. *That* she could deal with.

He stood up as she got to the table, and pulled out her chair. There were those manners again. He stroked his hand down her back. "I threw Drake out of the house."

"What?!" He couldn't be serious.

"I'm kind of teasing, and kind of not. He's an ox. He means well, but he's an acquired taste. Let's get some food in you."

"I'm really not hungry."

"Tell you what. Take a bite of everything on your plate, sips of milk in between. I even put the brownie on your plate."

She felt her lip twitch. Brownie. She really was hungry, who was she kidding? She needed protein. She'd been smelling those damn brownies in her car for over forty-five minutes.

"You're smiling. The potato salad is killer. Please, for me?"

He stroked the end of her nose. She loved that. It made her heart lurch every time he did it. She grinned and picked up her fork and scooped up some potato salad. "You're right. This is wonderful."

She watched as his blue eyes sparkled. "Now the turkey."

"I heard you the first time, Lieutenant. I'll eat a little, and then save room for barbeque, okay?"

"Okay."

"Gray are you hiding Riya?" Miranda called out.

"Stay here and eat. I'm going to keep out the riffraff." Gray got up and walked to the screen door to waylay Miranda.

Riya took small bites of her food, secure in the knowledge that she would have privacy.

"SHE'S AS TINY AS EVIE," Aiden said as he flipped one of the many steaks on the grill.

Gray looked up and saw Riya joining the ladies where they were seated underneath the umbrellas. Well, they weren't all ladies, there was also Dalton. He tended to hover around Aurora and their son, James.

"Is she settling in okay, or did my idiot brother-in-law scare the shit out of her?" Aiden turned down the flame on the grill.

"I thought she was going to hide under the kitchen table. But she seems to be settling in with Dalton."

Riya had taken the empty seat next to Dalton, and she was currently leaning in to listen intently to something he was saying. Aurora, Dalton's wife, leaned over him to say something to Riya, which had her smiling.

Good. Riya hadn't met Dalton before, so it was good to see her feeling so relaxed with him.

"Do you have any news on the women?" Aiden asked.

Gray knew immediately who he was talking about. "Chantelle is now home with her sister in Montreal. Chantelle sent a 'To Whom It May Concern' letter thanking us for saving her."

Aiden smiled. "She's good people." He flipped four

more steaks and put some hamburger patties on the grill.

"Are we going to see the letter?"

"It's already scanned and in your e-mails. I'm surprised Dex didn't bring a printed copy to the party."

Aiden shrugged. "What about Emily, the ambassador's daughter?"

"No word from any official channels. Wyatt did some digging. She's refusing therapy, and isn't talking."

"That's not good. Where are they? Did Ambassador Hoag ever come back to the states?"

Gray could hear Aiden's wheels turning.

"They're in Temecula. I think we should leave it for a while."

Aiden didn't say anything.

"Seriously, we need to take it easy," Gray counselled. "We don't own this."

"Remember what happened with Evie's sister, Chloe. This isn't something that you let fester."

Gray rubbed the back of his neck. "I'll think about it." He looked over at Riya. Now she was holding Dalton's son. It did his heart good to see her so comfortable.

"Oh my God, you have it bad," Aiden gloated.

"Huh?" Gray turned to look at his friend.

Aiden pointed his barbeque tongs at Riya. "You're looking at her exactly like I looked at Evie."

"At least I know I've got a good thing, and I don't have my head up my ass."

Aiden scowled at him. "Jesus, a man makes one mistake, and he never hears the end of it."

Gray raised an eyebrow, but he was smiling. It had

taken a hell of a long time for his friend to actually laugh about this, considering Evie almost lost her life because of that mistake. Aiden saved her, but the cost had been high.

"She's special," Gray said.

"Griff filled me in. Asperger's, right?"

What the fuck?

Gray stiffened, his focus went narrow. "That wasn't what I meant at all. I meant she means a lot to me. When did Griff say that? Did he say it just to you?"

"Calm down, Gray. He wasn't being unkind. As a matter of fact, he was highly complimentary about her. He just mentioned that she had Asperger's as well."

"What right does Griff have to lay some kind of label on Riya? Who the hell does he think he is? He's only met her a handful of times." But as soon as the words were out of his mouth, Gray knew the real culprit. It was Miranda, and he was furious. He saw Miranda talking to Piper Avery over near the dessert table.

"Gray, calm down." Aiden grabbed his arm.

Gray shoved Aiden's hand off. "Back off."

"I'm sorry I said anything." His second-in-command was seriously contrite.

Gray stalked across the yard. "Miranda, I need to talk to you for a minute."

She and Piper looked up at him in surprise. Then Miranda's eyes narrowed. "Piper, I'll be back to help set up the table."

"Let's go over to the birdbath behind the scheffleras, shall we?" Gray asked tightly.

"Sure." Miranda led the way, not saying a word.

When she got there she crossed her arms and looked up at Gray expectantly.

"Riya's supposed to be your friend. I can't believe you're talking behind her back."

"I need a better explanation of what you're talking about before I can respond."

It was clear how she could be an effective project manager dealing with high level members of the Pentagon.

"You're going around telling people Riya has Asperger's."

Miranda slowly nodded. "She does. A lot of the scientists I work with score somewhere on the autism spectrum, just like most SEALs score higher on the Extraversion and Conscientiousness scale than most people."

"I don't care about the Navy SEAL personality profile, I care about Riya."

He saw Miranda wave her hand and shake her head. Gray looked over his shoulder. He saw Griff barreling down on them. He nodded for him to join them.

"What's going on?" Griff demanded.

"You told Aiden that Riya had Asperger's."

"Fuck," Griff grimaced. "I just wanted him to be aware that she needed to be eased into the group. I didn't want her to be overwhelmed."

"She doesn't need some damn label hung around her neck," Gray bit out.

"Do you have a problem with Riya's diagnosis?" Miranda asked mildly. Her tone might be soft, but there was no mistaking the steel in her eyes.

"I have a problem with her being harmed by people thinking less of her."

"And do you?" Miranda's voice was even softer.

"Fuck no. She's perfect."

"Good answer, Big Man." Miranda's smile was bright.

"For the record, I don't require your approval," Gray said in his officer voice. Griff took a step in front of his wife, and Miranda pushed at her husband.

"Stay out of this Griff, you and your big mouth are in the doghouse. This is between Gray and me."

"Not likely," he growled. He turned to Gray. "I'm the one you're mad at, so talk to me, and quit badgering my wife. Not that she isn't perfectly capable of cutting off your balls and feeding them to you."

Even though he was pissed as hell, Gray couldn't hide a small smile.

"Gray, Riya was the one who told me about her condition," Miranda said easily. "That was almost two years ago when she first began working with me. She thought I needed to know. When she started to spend time at my house, I told Griffin." She rolled her eyes at her husband. "Most people on God's green earth have some kind of personality issue, including high-hand-ism, like you do, or big-mouthed-ism, like my husband. If we want to be frank, I seriously suffer from workaholism, and Griffin and Livvie have saved me from myself."

"Miranda, that's all well and good, but we all know that autism is a huge ass label, it's private."

"Goddammit, Gray, do you see anybody avoiding

Riya?" Griff asked incredulously. "Fuck no. This is us. You need to get a fucking grip."

"I—"

Griff grabbed his arm and pulled him past the schefflera. "Look. Do you see her?" He pointed to where Riya was now talking to Karen Avery and of all people, Drake Avery. "Does that look like someone who is being shunned? Fuck no."

Gray did a double take. Was that Drake leaning in with a gentle look on his face, holding his son out to Riya? He'd bet his bottom dollar that Aiden had said something to the man to get him to relax with Riya. It made him feel good to see that warmhearted interaction.

"Where's the trust, Gray?" Griff looked seriously confused.

Gray sighed. "You're right."

"Honey, he's in love, you need to cut him some slack."

Gray's gaze shot over to Miranda and saw her look of smug compassion. She put her hand on his arm. "I love the fact that you're in her corner, but you need to remember, so are we."

Gray looked back over at Riya. She and Drake were now laughing. Then a shaft of sunlight hit her, and she actually glowed. He sucked in a deep breath.

Love.

He loved her.

"Are we good?" Miranda asked softly.

"We're good."

12

RIYA SAT BACK AND LISTENED TO HER RADIO ABOUT someone dancing on their own. She used to feel that way, and instead she had an over-protective male who was going to be opening her car door any second.

Gray knocked on the window, and she unlocked her door, and he opened it.

"I like that your car was locked," he said as he took her hand and helped her out of the car.

"What's another word for over-protective?" Riya started walking with him up the path to her house.

"Caring?" he suggested.

She leaned against his side. When they got to the door, she fished out her keys and handed them to him. What was the point of fighting him on this? It was important for him to unlock the door and check her house. He went in and dealt with the alarm.

As soon as the door was shut behind them, he pulled her into his arms.

A slow burn had been building all day while she'd

watched him at the O'Malley's. Who was she kidding, it wasn't watching him, it was the way he cared for her. He made her feel cherished.

"I need my kiss," he rasped out.

"So who's stopping you?"

She loved teasing him.

He slanted his mouth over hers, and magic sparkled all around them. Her hands slid up his chest, kneading his hard muscles, reveling in his strength. He pulled her even closer, so that she was trapped. She didn't care, because his kiss had gone from a storm to a hurricane, ripping away all sense. Gray's hand was tangled in her hair, guiding her head so that her mouth was exactly where he wanted it.

Having Gray in charge aroused her. All of her erogenous zones flared to life. She squeezed her legs together to stop herself from squirming, but nothing could prevent the flame of heated response that gathered at her core.

Did he just bite my lower lip?

"Come back to me," he demanded. Then he pressed stinging kisses along her jaw and down the side of her neck.

Einstein tried to push himself between them, meowing his need for attention.

"Nope," Gray said looking down. "She's mine. You get her most of the time. Tonight she's mine."

Didn't that sound nice? Actually a whole lot better than nice. It sounded absolutely wonderful.

"Did you go away again?"

"Hmmm?" *What was he talking about?*

Gray was looking at her weird. He was waiting for her response.

"No, I was just thinking how I felt about your usage of the word 'mine'."

Gray winced. "And? What was your conclusion?"

"I liked it."

He backed her up against the hallway wall, hands on either side of her head. "That's good. Because you are. You're mine."

She had to tilt back her head to look at him. "What do I get to call you?"

He took his time answering. He moved one of his hands to cup her cheek, his rough thumb slid along her lower lip, sending shivers coursing through her body. "What do you want to call me? What do I mean to you?"

She'd been going to repeat back the word 'mine'. But then he asked that follow-up question. She hadn't quite anticipated this. Then, intellect melted into emotion, wave after wave of exquisite memories coursed through her body. She trembled with need, with passion but most of all, with love.

"You're my lover."

Gray went blank for a moment, then he gave her a wicked smile. "Damn right I am, let me take you upstairs and prove it."

He stepped backwards, and she grabbed his shirt with both hands. "No," she cried. "I said that wrong."

"What are you talking about? Of course I'm your lover."

"My love. You're my love, is what I meant to say."

Gray stopped, his sapphire blue eyes blazed. He covered her hands with his. "Honey—"

"I think I love you." The words burst out of her. They still weren't right. *Dammit.* Her fingers pressed into his chest through his sweatshirt. "I love you so much. You're my love. You're so much my love."

It was like the roof of her house had been ripped off, night turned to day and the sun was shining. She got it right. She loved Gray Tyler.

"Ah, Honey, that's what I meant when I claimed you as mine. I love you too."

RIYA'S EYES shimmered like black diamonds in the dim hallway light. He needed her in the most elemental way. He needed to stake his claim. Letting go of her hands he bent to pick her up, but she laughed and darted out from under him and made a run for it up the stairs. "Come and get me, Lover."

Oh, he was going to get her. Gray slowly made his way up the stairs. He saw that Riya had pulled back the comforter.

"Glad to see you hadn't taken off your clothes."

She pointed to her sneakers in the corner. Then she grinned. "I left my socks on, though. I've kind of figured out you like my feet."

The woman was right.

Scratch that, *his* woman was right.

Gray closed the bedroom door, and came to stand in front of her.

"Why'd you do that?"

"No company until sleepy time. Einstein puts me off my game."

"Gray, I have never complained. You have blown me away.

"Every.

"Single.

"Time."

That was actually great to hear, because she made him so crazy. He sometimes wondered if he was fucking things up when she was blowing his mind. He reached up and touched the strands of hair that covered her breasts. He gathered up the dark mass into a fist and enjoyed how she wet her lips in anticipation of what he would do next.

Pulling her hair into a ponytail at the back of her head, he tugged so that her face was tilted upwards. She gave a soft pant.

"You like this, don't you?"

"Yes." The word wasn't a sigh, it was a hiss.

He tugged harder. Her eyes dilated, and her face flushed. It still wasn't enough. He pulled just a little harder, and he exalted when he saw her squirm and squeeze her thighs together.

"You're wet for me, aren't you?"

She closed her eyes, then opened them. He couldn't tell where her pupils ended and her irises began. "I need you so bad. I'm so ready for you."

She couldn't say it. The woman who worked on a sex study couldn't admit she was wet. He swooped in for a kiss. It was hot and needy. She sent him close to the edge. No woman ever excited him more. He'd always thought love was going to be a soft and warm emotion, not this elemental, explosive craving.

Gray backed her up until he could lower her to the bed. As soon as she was lying down, he knelt at her feet and began to pull off her socks. She was right, he was obsessed with her feet. He stroked her arches.

"Hurry," she murmured.

"No."

He threw her socks over his shoulder, then he pulled her up into a sitting position. Ever so slowly, he peeled the UCSD sweatshirt over her head, then sucked in a deep breath when he found nothing but the sheerest red lace.

"Surprise," she whispered.

"You're going to give me a heart attack."

"I like wrapping paper, you like unwrapping gifts, it's a win-win." Her black eyes danced. He cupped her breasts while they were encased in the delicate fabric, then he circled her nipples with his thumbs. Riya threw her head back and moaned.

He put his mouth over one hard peak, and suckled.

"More," she cried.

He bit softly. It took him a moment to figure out she was trying to undo her jeans.

"Nuh-uh, that's my job." He pushed her back so that she was flat on her back. He divested her of her jeans. He took a short moment to admire the matching red thong, but right now it had to go.

"Please, Gray, hurry up."

He was going to do everything in his power, *not* to hurry up. But it was going to be hell. Riya struggled to sit up.

"What are you doing?"

"You're not hurrying. You need to be naked."

She was right.

"Lie back," he commanded sternly. She continued to move. He tried a different approach. "If you hold still, I'll make it worth your while."

All movement stopped, and her eyes glittered up at him. Damn, he was so hard, he'd never be able to unbutton his jeans over his erection. Gray pulled his Henley shirt over his head.

"More," she practically purred.

He sat down on the bed, and untied his boots, and yanked off his socks, then he stood back up and pulled at the buttons on his jeans, and winced. Yep, his woman had made the situation hard.

I did not just think that, did I?

His brain had officially turned to mush.

His.

She was his.

He picked up her foot and brought it to his chest. He stroked her toes, and looked at the flesh at the top of her thighs. He could see that she was wet for him, and it made him crazy. This petite little scientist matched him.

Riya gave him a sultry grin and slowly lifted her other leg, pointing her toe at him, as she aimed it at his erect flesh. Gray waited with baited breath, then she stroked her soft foot over his cock and he shuddered.

She gave him a wicked smile, then did it again, smoothing it up, then down. He grabbed her foot, pulling it away from his cock. He bent her legs and then knelt down beside the bed.

"No, it's my turn to taste you, I've been keeping score," she protested.

"You foolish, foolish girl. Keeping score means you think that I lose when I get to lick you up." Gray bent his head and gently brushed his tongue over her tender flesh. He heard her sigh with pleasure, and sweat gathered on the back of his neck. He wasn't going to last long.

"Get a condom," she breathed. As much as he wanted...needed...to hear that, he was going to make her come this way first.

Gray curled his tongue around the bud of her clit, then pushed a finger into her tight sheath. The feel of her was intoxicating. He needed to bury himself inside her. Her sighs were turning to moans. Gray increased the speed of his thrusts, and caressed her swollen flesh in tighter circles. More. Faster.

"Gray!"

Hallelujah.

He stood up and grabbed his jeans, fished out the condom and covered himself. Riya stared at him, clearly in a daze. He moved her languid body so that it rested in the middle of the bed, then slid beside her. He gathered her beside him. It was like a fire was lit, because Riya rolled over on top of him.

"Now I have you where I want you," She said.

"You do?"

The most perfect lips in the world lowered and blessed him with a kiss. Gray's head spun. He felt the rasp of lace on his chest, and realized the pretty red bra was still adorning Riya's golden flesh. He worked the clasp loose and slid it off her, so he could touch her luxuriant breasts without any impediment. He loved the feel of her stiff nipples rubbing against his palms. But there was one thing he needed more.

Gray lifted Riya and positioned her, so that he was lined up with her entrance. He looked up at her face. All he saw was eager anticipation. *Wasn't that fantastic?*

She braced herself against his abdomen and slowly slid downward, her tight flesh engulfing him in molten rapture. He gritted his teeth. It was her show, and he wasn't going to rush her, no matter how badly his body was demanding release.

"I want to do this forever and ever." He had to strain to hear her. When he did, his heart melted.

"So do I, Baby."

A long slide and he was home. "Help me, Gray." Another whisper.

"Tell me what you need, Riya."

She bent down, and rested her head on his chest. He slipped his hands down to the plush globes of her ass and pulled her close, starting a languid rhythm. Riya moved her hands and gripped his hair.

"God, yes. I need this. More, give me everything." She slammed her mouth to his, tangling their tongues, turning their lovemaking into a hectic force that stunned him.

Gray met her greedy need with masculine power. He rolled them over and Riya's legs clamped around his waist as her internal muscles milked his cock.

"Yes," she screamed out her release.

He closed his eyes as he followed her over the edge. He gathered her as close as he could. His universe could never be complete without her.

13

WHY IS GRAY'S SIDE OF THE BED COLD? RIYA PUSHED further and finally found warmth, but Einstein's fur wasn't the same thing as Gray's sleek flesh.

She pushed up on her pillow, then looked at the clock on her nightstand. Three o'clock in the morning? Where was Gray? Einstein butted his head against her arm. She gave him a few strong strokes. "You're nice and all, but I was really hoping for something yummier."

Riya got up and picked up all of her clothes and threw them in her laundry basket, then put on her sleepshirt, sweatpants and fuzzy socks. Hot chocolate sounded good. Maybe Gray had gotten hungry, but she doubted it, he would have been back by now. His pillow had been too cool and Einstein had been too comfy.

When she got halfway down the stairs she saw Gray sitting on the couch with his laptop. He must have brought it in from his car. She saw the glasses he was wearing and felt a tingle go through her body. He looked so distinguished. Then there was the hint of blond stubble. He was hot, with a capital 'H'.

Down girl.

And he'd said he loved her. She gripped the railing tighter.

"I hear you."

Gray didn't turn his head, he continued to concentrate on whatever was on the screen in front of him.

"I didn't make any noise. You couldn't have heard me," Riya protested.

"But I did. Why did you stop? Aren't you coming downstairs?"

She came down and sat next to him. He shut the laptop as she snuggled next to him. "Is it confidential?"

"'Fraid so."

"I was going to make cocoa, want some?"

"I don't have the chocolate tooth you do. I think I'll pass."

"Hot milk?" she asked.

"That sounds nasty."

She laughed as she got up from the couch and started for the kitchen. He followed her. He opened up the cupboard above the refrigerator and took out the antacid bottle.

"Old man, you need reading glasses and antacids?"

"You're supposed to respect your elders," Gray said as he leaned against the counter and watched her put a mug of water in the microwave. She ogled him out of the corner of her eye, but as she did she saw that he was looking at her oddly. She pulled the mug out and mixed the cocoa in.

"Gray, what's wrong?"

He sighed. That was odd. She didn't remember him being a man who sighed. She set the mug down on the counter.

"Darn it." She grabbed a paper towel and wiped up where some spilled because her hand had trembled.

"Riya, nothing's wrong."

"That's not true. You're acting funny."

He picked up her mug and set it on the kitchen bar, then pulled out a barstool for her to sit on. He sat beside her.

"Just tell me, Gray. I hate not understanding something."

He pulled her hands out of her lap, and held them. "Miranda said you suffer from Asperger's syndrome."

He was looking so concerned, she tried not to wince at his use of the word 'suffer'. Her heart started to beat fast. She took a deep breath. She tried to make sense of his expression. *Concerned, maybe? But what does it mean?*

"Okay, so she told you today? Why?"

"Aiden did. But Honey, the Asperger's isn't an issue. You know it isn't."

This totally didn't make sense. She blew out a stream of air. "Aiden? Aiden O'Malley?"

Gray's eyes grew stormy. "It was a clusterfuck. Miranda said something to Griff who talked to Aiden. They were just trying to make sure you felt comfortable. They wanted to make sure everyone was kind of laid-back."

Riya thought back to when she started at TAID. She'd been up front with Miranda that she was on the high-functioning end of the autism scale, that she basically had Asperger's. She explained that it shouldn't be a problem with her work, but that sometimes she was slow to clue in to some social situations. Miranda had been great in helping her out.

After six months she'd told Riya that she thought that a lot of times when she had trouble dealing with situations she thought it was her lack of work experience, not the Asperger's, and she should cut herself some slack. She could tell that Miranda had studied up on the diagnosis and worked hard to assist her on the job. Riya had been overjoyed to find such a great mentor.

"Why is it a clusterfuck if they were just trying to be nice?" She had to be missing something. "It's a good thing, isn't it?"

"They had the best intentions. My friends have great hearts, I just don't want you to feel uncomfortable."

"Is that why you're up in the middle of the night?"

"Partly. I was also checking up on some things from our last mission."

She studied his face, trying to get a read on him, at the same time trying to figure out how she felt that people had to be told to make her feel comfortable.

"How awkward was it for your friends?"

"Huh?" Gray twined his fingers between hers so that their palms met. "Oh. Shit, Riya. Jack, one of our former teammates who wasn't there today, damn near called a team meeting to tell us how to behave before we met Beth. He thought she needed to be handled like spun-glass."

"Did she?"

"Maybe in the beginning," Gray admitted. "I think Griff only told Aiden. who more than likely told Evie about you."

Riya thought through the day's events. "Dalton. They told Dalton. He was really calm and gentle."

Gray gave a wistful smile. "Dalton has his own story, so no, that's just the way he is."

"Then I don't understand. Why are you so upset if the host and hostess were told I needed to be eased into a social situation? I know some people are bothered by this, but they didn't seem to be. I mean, I can explain it to you. It's really a lot more common than you'd think. Wait, I have a book on it, let me go get it." She tried to pull her hands out of his grip, but he wouldn't let go.

"Calm down, I don't need a book."

A book? Had I really offered a book? What a dumbass. Wait a minute...

"Are *you* weirded out, now that you know?"

He reared back and looked at her askance. "Are you seriously asking me that question?"

She looked at him and relaxed. "I guess I shouldn't have worried."

"Damn right you shouldn't. I love you. I love every single thing about you, even your wrapping paper fetish."

She tightened her fingers on his. "I'll handle time with your friends better as I get to know them."

"Hell yeah you will. I've watched you handle everything. Hell, you even managed to conquer Drake Avery at the end."

She snorted. "It was easy as soon as he got around his wife, then he got all gooey."

Gray let go of her hands, draping his arms around her neck and rubbed his nose against hers. "And me? When do I get all gooey?"

"My man? He doesn't get gooey, he gets hard."

Nothing was better than Gray Tyler's laughter.

"Riya?"

She wrote a note, then shut off her microscope and looked over at the door of Jonah's lab, where she'd been hiding.

"Hey Susan," she smiled.

"You have your cell phone turned off again."

Riya sighed. She fished out her phone from her lab coat and realized it was powered off. "It was ringing too much. I'm on a deadline."

"There's a pissed off general in Miranda's office. She's been holding him off, but I think she needs your help. What are you doing in here? We've been looking all over for you."

Riya turned on her phone as she quickly walked over to Susan. "Shit, there's a ton of texts, and they're not just from Miranda. What's going on?"

"I don't know. But you're a popular girl. The CDC has been calling for you, too."

"I'm sorry, I was hiding in here to get this last set of tests done. Jonah took today off, and he keeps a tight ship, so leaving my lab was worth it to finish up. I'm sorry, Susan."

They went out the door and across the campus to Miranda's office. When they got there, she saw

Lieutenant General Astor drinking coffee and laughing at something Miranda was saying.

"There you are," Miranda smiled. "The general told me how impressed he was with your work last month. Of course he didn't go into as much detail as I would have liked." Miranda waved her to the seat beside the general.

Well she had done a good job, but she sure didn't remember the general singing her praises. It must have been more of the Porter magic.

"Dr. Patel, it's good to see you again." He cleared his throat. "She and I were reviewing your file. When you took your job with TAID and got your clearances with the government, it was with the understanding you might be asked to work on classified and / or top secret assignments."

"Yes, I remember. It also said that the assignments were at my discretion."

Riya thanked God that the leather seat she was sitting in had high arms, it allowed her to slip her hands under her legs to contain the sweat forming on her palms.

"Riya, I think you understand that if we asked you to work on something that was top secret it was because your country needed you. I talked to everyone at the Pentagon, and I was told you were the man for the job. I mean, woman."

When things were this confusing, she found it was just better to wait, and let the person speaking to just keep talking, so she waited.

"We have a top secret international assignment. It's critical that you go on this mission. Your country needs you." His eyes drilled into hers, it took every ounce of her willpower not to drop her gaze. "Will you do this?"

She sat up straighter. "Of course I will."

"Good." He gave a brisk nod.

"General, when will this assignment begin? Is there something that Dr. Patel can review prior to leaving?" Miranda asked.

"She'll be leaving out of NAS tonight. When she reaches Coronado she'll join the briefing with the team. Members of the CDC will be meeting us there with the equipment she'll need."

Suddenly she wasn't as worried. He was talking her language. "What kind of equipment, Sir?"

"She'll need a portable biocontainment lab." He spoke to Miranda instead of her.

Riya looked over at Miranda and did a quick eyeroll that the general couldn't see. Then she turned back to him.

"Understood, General. I'll be dealing with at least a BSL-1 safety hazard, got it. Is it the same one I was researching before? The airborne contagion?"

"Are you excited about this?" It sounded like he was angry. No, it was more like he had eaten something he didn't like. It took her a moment to figure out what he was thinking.

"I take my projects very seriously. I think you are misunderstanding my eagerness to assist you, with some sort of elation."

"Oh. Well then," he smiled. She could tell she had appeased him. "Riya, I'm grateful to have you working on this. I'm just sorry I didn't have you continue working on the contagion longer, like you wanted too."

Having dealt with enough Pentagon personnel, she knew better than to smile at this point. But inside she was smiling. Inside she was thankful that she had continued to analyze the contagion and come to some of her own conclusions. Maybe this would give her a leg up on whatever job she would be doing.

"MASON, do you have any idea what this is about?" Gray asked his counterpoint, the lieutenant of the Midnight Delta SEAL team.

"I'm as much in the dark as you are," Mason responded.

They looked up as the conference room door opened.

"Hey, guys," Max Hogan nodded his head.

"Well, this has to be big, if they pulled you in from Virginia. Did they bring in your entire team?" Gray asked the lieutenant of the Night Storm SEAL team.

"Yep. We just got in an hour ago," he said, taking a seat at the table. He looked tired.

"Weren't you just on an op in Bolivia?" Mason asked.

Max waved his hand. "Something like that. We got home five days ago. We're ready for something new."

"Kane was a real help to us on our last mission," Gray said. "I really appreciated that."

Max gave a wan smile. "Don't think Dex and Clint haven't returned the favor."

The door opened and Commander Liam McAllister and Captain Josiah Hale walked in the room. Shit, this had to be big if they were bringing in all three teams, and the captain was the one briefing them.

Captain Hale walked to the head of the conference table and pressed his fists down on the polished surface. He leaned in, his expression grave. "In just a second, men, Lieutenant General Astor of the United States Marine Corp will be walking in here with three scientists. The long and short of it is, we have a major clusterfuck on our hands, and it's related to the mission Black Dawn was on last month. When the assignments are doled out, I'm sending Gray's team and the most experienced scientist to the most likely hotspot. Then we'll—"

The door opened. "Sorry I'm late. Hello everybody. I'm Lieutenant General Astor." He held the door open and in walked Riya followed by two men.

Gray stood up, and Mason grabbed his arm. "Riya?" Gray's voice was incredulous.

"Do you two know one another?" General Astor asked, as Riya, the general and two men sat down on the opposite of Gray and the other two SEAL lieutenants.

Riya's face showed no expression.

"Dr. Patel?" The general turned to look at her.

"Yes, I know Lieutenant Tyler. Miranda Porter is married to one of his men."

Captain Hale cleared his throat. "This could be convenient. Let me introduce my men. Lieutenant Gray Tyler is in charge of Black Dawn. His team completed the mission in Al Khobar last month."

"Damn good work," the general said.

Gray gave a sharp nod. He kept his focus on his

captain, he couldn't handle looking at Riya, everything was too surreal.

"Mason Gault is in charge of Midnight Delta."

"I've heard of your team," the general smiled at Mason. Then he turned to Max. "You command the Night Storm team, right?"

"Yes Sir," Max nodded.

"What have you told your men?" the general asked Captain Hale.

"Not much," the captain said as he stood at the front of the table. "I was waiting for you to arrive."

"Good. Who's this?" The general nodded toward Liam.

"This is Commander Liam McAllister. He'll be coordinating the three teams while they're out in the field."

The general grinned for the first time since he came into the room. "Your reputation proceeds you, McAllister. Seems like you've pissed some people off lately."

Liam didn't say anything, but his smile was shrewd. While the general and Liam had a mini-bromance, Gray tried to get Riya's attention, but she was busy folding the corner pages of her black composition notebook. She might not show any expression on her face, but her nervous tic showed she was as stunned by this turn of events as he was.

"Have a seat, men," the general said to Hale and McAllister. After they were seated, he looked around the conference table. "Gentlemen, and Lady, we have a problem that is going down in the next twenty-four to thirty-six hours according to our sources at Langley.

Someone very close to the upper echelons of the Saudi royal family is planning something big. They've been dealing with a lot of negative international media attention which has turned into some instability within the family. It's creating a power struggle. Our CIA source, who is exceedingly reliable, says that the Prince is planning something in less than two days."

The Middle East, like that was something new. But the idea of Riya being part of something with the Saudi royal family made his blood cold. He tried to get her attention, but her gaze was fixated on her notepad.

"You think the Saudis are responsible for creating that contagion?" Riya asked the general.

"Yes. Our team was able to analyze the delivery system used in the proof of concept they pulled in Las Vegas. It has the same signature as one the Saudis used with a nerve agent in Yemen."

"What proof of concept?" Liam asked.

"That'll be explained at the overall meeting," the general said. "In here, I want to go over what Langley said and the team assignments."

"There is a tech conference in Dubai, a fashion show in Bahrain, and a humanitarian award ceremony in Abu Dhabi. Every single one of these is a viable target, but we've identified the most people the Saudis might want to take out, at the Abu Dhabi event."

There was a ringing sound, and the general pulled out his phone.

"I need to take this," he said as he got up and went to the corner of the conference room.

"Why do we need scientists?" Gray said looking at Captain Hale.

The general put his phone back into his pocket. "Good question. I'll handle that explanation when we're with you and your entire teams. Where are they?"

"We have all of our men assembled together down the hall," Mason said.

"Great. We'll go meet with them," the general said as he stood up. "The CIA thinks all three targets have a high likelihood of being hit, but I'm convinced it's going to be the humanitarian award ceremony in Abu Dhabi. There are five or six high profile targets that the Saudis are salivating to take out." He pointed at Gray. "Since your team just handled Al Khabor, I want Black Dawn there." He turned to Captain Hale. "Captain, who do you want on the other two assignments?"

Captain Hale gave Gray's counterparts considering looks. "Max, you're Bahrain. Mason, you're taking Dubai."

The general started talking again. He turned to Liam. "We'll follow you, Commander to the meeting room." He motioned for Riya and the other two scientists to follow him out of the room. Riya kept her head down as she left.

"Fan-fucking-tastic, we get to babysit a bunch of models in Bahrain. Seriously, put a bullet in me," Max said under his breath.

"Aren't you single?" Mason asked Max, as Gray watched Riya's braid swing behind her while she walked out the door.

"Yep," Max answered. "And when I was younger, I dated models. These days I'd prefer to dress in a chicken suit and carry one of those billboards in Times Square."

God, could these two clowns take any longer to get out of the room?

"Speed it up, I need to get to the briefing." Gray growled at Max.

"What's up with you and the pretty scientist?" Mason asked.

"If you'd get out of my way, I can tell them that the pretty scientist isn't qualified to go on a mission."

Max and Mason stopped, blocking his way. Mason pushed a hand into his chest. "What the fuck are you thinking?"

"Riya is mine, and she sure as hell isn't going on a mission to some sort of hotspot. No way, no how."

"Man, you have no choice." Max's voice was implacable.

"Watch me." He pushed past Mason and Max and yanked open the conference room door.

14

THE GENERAL HAD GIVEN HER NO INDICATION REGARDING the mission on the short drive from the TAID headquarters to Coronado. But he was sure willing to pepper her with questions regarding the contagion she had examined while at the Pentagon lab.

"You had said that it was possible to funnel down the contagion so that it could target an ethnicity and maybe even get to the point where it could be specific enough to focus in on a sickle cell carrier, right?"

It had taken a few moments for Riya to respond because she hadn't thought the general had been listening to her when she'd been in D.C.

"That's right."

"Could it get to the point where the poison could be sprayed in or delivered through an air duct, and just be directed at certain family members?"

Riya felt her pulse rate increase. "Absolutely."

"This isn't just a theory?" His eyes left the road, and he peered over at her.

"No, it isn't just a theory. That contagion was elegant in its design, and it was on its way to surpassing anything I have seen before. Whoever has developed it is a genius."

"Smarter than you? Because everything I've read, and everything I've been told, is that you are a wunderkind. There's nobody better."

That stopped her up short. She knew she was good. Brilliant even. But the best?

"I don't know, General," she said honestly.

"I'm hoping that you're not needed. If things go right, you won't be. But it's possible we're going to need your brain. And if we do, you have to be smarter than this asshole. Got it?"

What is going on?

"All I can do is try," Riya answered.

"That's not good enough." She saw his knuckles turn white as he gripped the steering wheel. "You better damn well succeed."

So here she was walking into a huge room filled with big men, some of whom she'd met, all of them looking grim, and she could feel Gray behind her back. She might have trouble reading people, but there was no mistaking the fact that he was beyond angry.

"Take a seat," the man who had done the introductions said. He gestured to her and the two other CDC scientists to sit down in the front row. She watched as the other two SEAL team lieutenants went to the back of the room, but Gray sat down right beside her, his body vibrating with rage. She wanted to run away, or cry. Actually she wanted to do both. But then she looked at the general at the front of the room. He was staring directly at her.

"Okay everybody, listen up," he started. "I've brought you together because we have a big problem."

She heard someone mumble behind her. "Like that's new." He sounded amused.

"Your lieutenants will inform you of the mission specifics, they're being sent to us from Langley. On a high level, they are in three high profile events in Dubai, Abu Dhabi and Bahrain."

"We have extremely reliable intel that a poison is going to be used on at least one if not more specific targets and that it is sanctioned by the higher echelons of the Saudi royal family. If we were to give a heads up to either the governments of Bahrain or the U.A.E., there would be a massive shitstorm. Therefore the analysts out of Langley have determined, along with your Captain, that your three teams can handle this."

"Fuck yeah," that same quiet voice mumbled.

Riya raised her hand.

"Dr. Patel?" The general pointed at her.

"You're talking about the same contagion that I examined last month, correct?"

He nodded.

"Are you sure it can be amplified to large enclosed spaces?" she asked.

"Yes. Did you hear about the Llewellyn triplets who were rushed to the hospital from the nightclub in Las Vegas two nights ago?"

"Who?" she asked.

The general grimaced. "My thought exactly. They're some YouTube sensation. Anyway, they died.

Their deaths had all the hallmarks of meningitis. As soon as it was flagged, the CDC got involved and we got involved. We knew it was the same poison used in Al Khabor. The nightclub was twelve-thousand square feet. Those were the only three people impacted."

Holy crap.

"Holy shit," a man said behind her.

"Dr. Patel, since you researched this contagion, would you please come up and explain the significance of the triplets being the only ones affected."

Riya stood up and went to the lectern. She rifled through the pages in her notebook. Giving a presentation wasn't new, but having to give it when cold blue eyes were glaring at her made her knees shake.

Just keep your eyes on the page.

"When I first examined —"

"Louder," someone yelled from the back.

She looked up and saw Gray, her gaze skittered away from him, and she saw Drake Avery. He gave her a sweet smile of encouragement. It helped. She cleared her throat.

"When I first examined this, I thought it was a toxin, because I only had a sample of cloth. There were microscopic particles of the airborne poison that was actually a contagion. I soon realized it carried a fast-acting form of meningitis, something that had never been developed before. In speed, it is along the line of Ebola or ricin. After comprehensive testing, it was clear that it only impacted the Y chromosome, i.e. men. What's more, the way it was developed, the person who was targeted was not contagious."

She looked up and saw that everybody in the room was nodding their heads.

"It was clear to me that even though it was used as a poison, that this kind of specific virus could be developed further so that it could target specific gene pools. If that could happen, why not reverse it so instead of a poison, turn it into a treatment for things like sickle cell anemia?"

Again, she looked up. She was surprised by the number of heads that were still nodding. She shouldn't have been. She'd read enough SEAL books to know that intelligence was part of the selection criteria. God knew Gray was brilliant.

"Dr. Patel, does this poison have to be DNA specific, or could it be used on a broad population?" Liam McAllister asked.

"The thing that makes this so extraordinary is that they can target DNA. In theory, yes Commander, they could use this contagion on the masses. But what would be the point?" she answered.

Now came the part where she needed to come clean with the general. "When I left the lab in D.C. I continued to work on the specific sequencing of the contagion. It was intriguing. As I reversed engineered the sequence —"

"What?" the general said in a deep voice. "Would you mind repeating that Dr. Patel?"

What was he going to do, send her home? Not bloody likely.

"I said that after I left D.C. last month I doodled with the sequencing of the contagion from memory. It was important work that couldn't be shoved into some corner. Lucky for us I was able to reverse engineer some of the bacteria's sequence and calculate—"

"Doc," she looked up and saw Drake Avery with his hand up.

"Yes?"

"Are you saying you figured out a way to stop the poison?" Drake asked in a friendly voice.

"It's not a poison. It's a bacteria. It's a contagion. It's not caused because you breathe it and it poisons you, it causes you harm because it prevents your body from functioning. Then your body begins to deteriorate. The difference between a poison and a contagion is-"

"So can you stop the toxin?" he asked hopefully.

She sighed. "Toxin isn't the right word either," she winced.

Drake smiled easily. "Got it. Contagion."

"So have you figured out a way to stop the contagion even after it's been sprayed?" Gray's voice was biting.

"If I get to the victims fast enough, I think I can, because the aerosol shouldn't have hit them with an intense enough dose to kill them immediately." She turned to the general. "I'm assuming these triplets took at least twelve hours to die, and that none of the normal treatments for meningitis worked?"

He gave her a surprised look. "How did you know?"

"It's how I would have progressed the contagion after a month. What they had developed last month was in its early stages."

"Do you have notes that we can review?" one of the CDC scientists asked.

"I'll scan them and e-mail you copies," she offered.

"No," Commander McAllister said. "We'll make copies here, and provide them to you. I don't want things on unsecure e-mail servers."

"Mine is secure," Riya protested.

"I'm not talking about yours, Dr. Patel," Liam said as he nodded toward the two CDC scientists.

"I need you to break into your teams and go over your specific plan details," the captain said. "Dr. Patel, you're going to Abu Dhabi with Black Dawn since they're assigned to the most likely target and you're the one most familiar with the contagion. I trust the fact that you are familiar with members of that team will only be a plus."

He wasn't looking at her, he was staring at Gray.

"Captain, may I talk to you?" Gray asked.

"No," he said. "Dismissed." He started walking out of the briefing room. The general paused at the lectern.

"You walked a very fine line, Dr. Patel. A very fine line. Do you understand me?"

She gulped. "Yes Sir."

"If something like this happens again, you won't find me so understanding, do you comprehend me?"

"Yes Sir."

He left the briefing room.

Commander McAllister stayed behind. "Max, hit the Conference Room C. Mason, you're in One over in the annex building. Gray, you and your team will stay here with me."

Riya watched as Max tapped one of the scientists on their shoulder. Apparently they were interchangeable.

Lucky them.

She watched through her bangs as the lieutenant

named Mason escorted the other scientist out of the room. Soon she was left with Gray, Liam and the five other SEALs she'd already met. *Well thank God for small miracles, at least I can put names to faces.*

"Liam, can I speak to you in the hall?" Gray's voice was a subdued roar. She jerked her head down so that the only thing she could see were her notes. Riya heard the door click. Her lip hurt, she tasted copper.

"Riya?"

It was Aiden O'Malley. She couldn't look up. She couldn't.

"Honey, Gray's behaving like an ass. You need to ignore him."

She turned another page in her notebook, and pressed down the corner. Uh-oh, she needed to stop doing that. They needed to be flat so they could be scanned. She wasn't doing anything right.

"Let me. You guys take off. I don't give a shit if you interrupt Gray and Liam." Aiden sounded angry.

Oh no, another harsh voice.

She heard footsteps, and then the door closed again. A man's big hand slowly pulled the notebook out of her grasp. She had no choice but to look up. Aiden had a compassionate smile on his face.

"Honey, you need to quit biting your lip."

She touched it and winced.

Then all of her emotions, her questions, bubbled out, in a forlorn cry.

"Why is Gray so mad at me? I don't understand."

Riya was horrified when she felt a tear track down her face. She never, ever cried. Not ever.

Aiden walked to her side of the lectern and pulled

her trembling frame into his arms. "He's angry because he's scared to fucking death."

"That makes no sense at all," she choked the words into the front of his olive green t-shirt. She sucked in a deep breath then pushed out of his arms.

No, this wasn't right at all.

"Aiden, my country needs me. This contagion might behave like meningitis, but it isn't. It's something else. I've almost got it. If I can analyze the pure form, I can reverse the virus before it gets to the lethal stage."

"Those are some pretty big 'ifs'," Aiden said.

"Yes they are," Gray said.

Riya whirled around to see Gray and Commander McAllister standing in the doorway.

"If we do our job right, it's never going to come to that, now is it?" Aiden asked his Lieutenant in a steely voice.

"The reason we send you out on these missions is because they're fluid. It's up to you to make sure the bad guys are stopped." Liam's voice held just as much steel as Aiden's. "Dr. Patel, Gray has put in a formal protest for you not to be on this mission. What is your decision?"

All three sets of eyes were on her. She kept her gaze on the Commander. "This is my area of expertise. Nobody knows more about this contagion than I do. I promised the general I would do it, not because it's in my field, but because I needed to be involved. I *have* to help my country, just like the three of you have been doing for years."

"Then you're going with Gray and his men." He pushed open the door. "Get your asses back in here," he called out. In seconds, Wyatt, Dalton, Dex and Griff filed into the room.

IT HAD BEEN a hell of a long flight to Abu Dhabi, and Gray hadn't said a word to Riya the entire time. He'd been busy with Dex, and she'd been on her laptop furiously going over information coming in from Las Vegas, that she was sharing with the two other CDC scientists. The truck spit them out at one of the myriad of buildings on the Al Dhafra Air Base. It would have seemed like dream weather compared to what it had been in Saudi Arabia last month if it weren't for the fact that his blood pressure was through the roof.

For fuck's sake, part of the million dollars' worth of training the good ole U.S. of A had given him was meditation and relaxation techniques to do when in stressful situations, but nothing had prepared him for this. He watched as Wyatt helped Riya out of the truck and he and Griff flanked her as they headed for the building that housed officer quarters.

On the flight over from NAS to the United Arab Emirates, he'd devoured every bit of information he could on the contagion, the delivery system and Dr. Riya Patel. How the fuck hadn't he realized just who he was in love with? He'd known she was a genius, but he hadn't realized she was the highest ranking fucking figure in this field of study. Hell, she was on track to win major awards, maybe even the Nobel. Thank God she was a little clumsy and awkward at times, otherwise he might be too intimidated to touch her again.

Gray winced as Wyatt grabbed Riya's arm when she stumbled. He looked at the ground and saw nothing but flat surface where she was walking. God he loved his woman. He shoved out of the truck. Goddammit, he needed to be the one assisting her when she tripped over nothing.

"I've got her," he said as he caught up to the trio.

Griff gave him the stink-eye.

"It's okay Gray —" Wyatt started.

"I want to walk with Gray," Riya interrupted Wyatt. "I'll meet you inside."

"Wyatt, work with Dex to have everything set up when Riya and I get in there. I want to go over the plans one last time," Gray instructed his subordinate.

Wyatt nodded. Griff continued to stand there next to Riya.

"Porter, do you need an engraved invitation to leave?" Gray snarled.

"If you're going to be this much of an asshole to me, then yes. I'm not leaving her alone with you."

Riya straightened to her full height of five foot nothing and looked Griff straight in the eye. "It's fine. Your lieutenant and I need to get a couple of things straightened out before this mission takes place. I want to make sure that the wax has finally been cleared from his ears, otherwise things could go badly."

Gray cringed as Griff laughed. "Riya, I think you've been taking lessons from my wife. Good for you."

Gray watched as Griff gave her arm a quick squeeze before he sauntered off to the building.

She crossed her arms and looked up at him, her eyes squinting in the sun. "So talk."

"I don't want you to go on this mission."

She rolled her eyes. "Try to say something less obvious."

Who was this woman, and why was his dick getting hard?

"Dalton and Aiden just carried in a portable biocontainment unit and blue suit. Jesus, Riya, this shit will kill you dead in under an hour if you get too close to it."

"And that would be why positive pressure protective suits were invented." She continued to look him in the eye. "Look, Gray, I think your plan is a good one, if, and this is a pretty big if, the Saudis choose the humanitarian award ceremony here in Abu Dhabi and if they actually use one of the air ducts on the roof like you think they will. Then there is a high probability you will stop them."

And if that didn't work, he and his team would normally come up with a different plan to save the world, that's what they were trained to do. But tonight one of his fail-safes involved putting a civilian in play. Not just any civilian, either. A woman. *His* woman.

"There is still the unlikely, but possible chance they could just set the timer-controlled canister in the ballroom and leave," she said.

"Do you think I haven't thought of that?" Gray thought his jaw would shatter as he tried not to yell.

"You didn't mention it on the plane," she reminded him softly.

"It was one of the items Dex put down on his list of possibilities. We're not all going to be on the roof, Riya. That's not how we work."

The hot morning wind started kicking up dust. Gray had sunglasses on, Riya didn't. "Come on Honey, let's get you inside before you melt." He gently touched her elbow. She jerked away from him.

"No! You can't all of a sudden be nice. It's too confusing. You're still mad, aren't you?" she accused.

He looked at the building that was fifty meters away. Once they were inside, they wouldn't have any privacy. He turned her around so he blocked the wind. "Riya, I sure as hell hope you know I love you."

She looked like she was going to cry.

Fuck. Had he really blown it that badly?

"Riya. Let me state it loud and clear. I fucking love you. That's why I don't want you to go. Hell, I really don't want those CDC motherfuckers on this mission, but I'd take them in a minute instead of you."

She flinched, and turned on her heel.

Holy mother of God, he was sounding like Drake Fucking Avery.

"Riya, stop. Goddammit, please stop. I'm wrong. I'm dumb. I'm sorry." He ran in front of her and gently put his hands on her shoulders to stop her from moving forward. Fucking-A, she was crying now.

"I cannot believe the amount of dumb crap that is falling out of my mouth." He took a deep breath. He shoved his sunglasses up on his head and bent down so they were eye to eye.

"Number one, I love you. Say yes if you understand."

She didn't answer for a long time, but her tears dried up. "The Gray from yesterday loved me. I don't know this Gray."

"That brings us to number two. I'm scared to fucking death that something bad will happen to you. Scared to death." He prayed she could read the truth in his eyes, but she was looking down.

"Please Riya, look at my face. Look into my eyes. See that I'm telling you the truth."

"No, you've been mad at me."

She looked lost and confused.

"I've been mad at this situation. And terrified that you could die. I love you to pieces, I want you in my life forever. I would fall apart if something bad happened to you."

She shoved him in his chest so hard he fell back a step. "You dumbass, you mean to tell me that when you feel protective, you're going to act like a pissy asshole? I can't believe this!"

He jumped forward and grabbed her in a hug. "Now you get it. Am I forgiven?" he begged with a hopeful grin.

"I don't want to get it. I want you to behave like a logical human being," she wailed. "But yes, you're forgiven."

"I told you that the SEAL quirks were worse than your quirks any day of the week."

"Gray, you have to take me seriously. I'm part of this."

There weren't enough antacids in the world to handle this situation. But...

"Riya, me and my men are going to do everything possible so you don't have to touch that contagion, but if push comes to shove and you have to suit up? Well, you're the scientist I trust the most to handle things."

"You're not just saying that?"

"Absolutely not. Riya, I've watched you take on every obstacle and succeed, of course you'll handle this with ease."

She laughed. "Yeah, well you're a superhero, I won't have to do anything."

He sure as hell hoped she was right.

Please God, let her be right.

15

WEARING A LITTLE BLACK COCKTAIL DRESS WAS NOT WHAT she anticipated when she thought about going on a mission with a SEAL team.

Talk about bizarre.

"Be careful with that," Wyatt said to the two bellhops who were lugging the two large cases that contained her portable biocontainment lab. Another bellhop had a cart that was filled to the top with suitcases.

"Riya, you need to cut back on the shoes," Wyatt teased. "The luggage fees are out of control, Darling."

Riya had no idea how to respond to that, so she kept her mouth shut. Wyatt was wearing Navy dress whites, as he escorted her to the hotel elevator. They were supposedly a couple checking into the awards ceremony that was supposed to start in two hours.

Wyatt was with her because he was still not battle ready, so he would be manning logistics and communications. She was pretty sure that he'd really been brought to Abu Dhabi to babysit her.

As soon as Wyatt had tipped the bellhops and they were alone in their room, he threw all the suitcases on the beds and quickly started opening everything up.

"Just how many guns did you bring?" Riya asked.

"You can never have enough fire power," Wyatt said, not bothering to look up. He continued to open suitcase after suitcase. Finally he opened the one that contained her positive pressure protective suit, and everything she would need inside the biocontainment lab.

"What is all of that?" Wyatt asked as he booted up his computer.

"This is a centrifuge and that is a thermal cycler." Riya continued to unwrap items from the bubble wrap. "Hold on and I'll tell you what the rest of the equipment is."

"No, Riya. I don't need you to tell me what the name is of each piece of equipment. I want to know what you plan to do with them. I mean, I'm not going to tell you this is a MP7 submachine gun, you just need to know it goes bang. For example, what the hell does all this do?"

"The thermal cycler will amplify segments of the DNA, that will assist me in isolating what is relevant." She bit her lip. "Actually, I pray to God that your team finds the canister before it opens and emits anything. If it's closed, we still know it's on a timer to open and emit the vapor, so we've got to get it into a containment system."

"We've got that covered," Wyatt pointed to the five oxygen cylinders. "They're empty, and they've been modified. Using the canister that was found at the nightclub in Vegas as a template, two mechanics in San Diego made these up from our oxygen tanks. We can drop in the 'live' poison canisters and dispose of them at our leisure."

"They're not live until the two gel packs inside the canisters dissolve and the liquids inside the packs mix and form the gas."

"Yeah, Riya, you explained that the gel packs will dissolve within an hour, so they have to time this just right. But what I don't get is why it matters, once the canister is filled with the gas, can't they just let it sit there forever, before opening it up?"

"They recovered the canister in Las Vegas where the toxic gas was held."

"I know," Wyatt said. "That's what we based our safety containers on."

"Well, that canister is too small to house the gas for long, maybe a half-hour at the most, before the gas will revert to liquid."

Wyatt frowned, "but it's still poisonous, right?"

"Oh, it's deadly in that concentrated liquid form," she confirmed. "It's just not an aerosol, which is a good thing."

"When it hits the air, will it go back to its aerosol form?" Wyatt asked.

"No, the original interaction that occurred between the two is what created the gas. We're good once it goes liquid. It's that first fifteen minutes that we're screwed."

"Not a problem," Wyatt said with a grin. "We'll get the guys, and contain the shit, before it farts."

It took her a moment to figure out what farting had to do with what they were talking about. When she did, she giggled. Riya felt one of the boulders fall off her shoulders.

Wyatt reminded her of the UCSD soccer player she tutored for a semester. He'd been hard for her to understand to begin with, because he'd always been goofing around, but in the end she'd realized it was important to him to earn her respect and be her friend. They still talked at least once a quarter. Yep, if she really spent time and studied Wyatt she bet he would turn out to be the same way.

"Riya? Are you okay? You're kind of spacing out on me."

"I'm sorry, I do that sometimes."

Time to stop reminiscing.

"Here's what needs to happen. We need to measure the bathroom, and see if the lab will fit in there after we get it open," she said decisively.

"Already ahead of you. I checked out the room specs before reserving the room. That's one of the reasons I ponied up for the Palace Suite. The containment lab will fit when it's unfolded."

"Good, that's good. The suitcases the lab comes in actually turn into tables, so that's easy enough to set up. Then I put this equipment in there."

"Do you take that with you everywhere?"

"What?" she asked.

Wyatt pointed to her black and white college notebook.

"Oh, I go through these like water. This is the one I started using when I came home from D.C. last month." She went over to him and he moved two of the guns so she could sit beside him on the bed. "Here's the sequencing that they did on the contagion last time." She pointed to a page excitedly, then turned many pages forward. "But here's a sample of what they took off the triplets. Can you see the difference?"

She looked up expectantly, and Wyatt gave her a crooked grin. "Doc, I'm not anywhere close to understanding that. I'm really honored you think I might have had a snowball's chance in hell of comprehending it though."

Riya felt the blush starting from her toes and ending at her forehead. Of course he didn't know anything about this. Nobody but the other CDC scientists would have known. She was just so excited to share this with someone. At least Gray would have realized the importance of her differentiating between the two different samples. That was huge!

"Hey, don't go feeling all bad. You should see the stupid shit I pull. It's mostly with women."

She laughed. *How can I not, when he is so dang cute?*

He got up from the bed and within five minutes had the biocontainment lab set up in the hotel's luxurious bathroom. The CDC's soft-walled lab came with a portable generator that powered the HEPA filtration system. Wyatt even had it worked out so she would step into the bathroom's tub to scrub down between the two doorways of the biocontainment lab, so that she wouldn't track any of the particles to the outside. Again, it shouldn't be a problem, since it would be DNA specific, but it was still a good protocol to have.

"Riya, you're kind of weird, do you know that?" Wyatt asked.

"Yeah, I do. But why are you saying it?"

"This bathroom has a whirlpool tub, a sauna, a steam room, and a huge vanity for you to sit down at, but you could care less. I cover it all up with aluminum and plastic and you're a kid in a candy store. You're just weird."

Riya clapped her hands and grinned. "I know."

Wyatt handed her a small earpiece. She looked at it, and twirled it around in her hand until she determined how to put it into her ear. Then he handed her something to go around her neck.

"It's a throat microphone. It works better than the ones you see the kids using to play video games. You can whisper, and we'll hear you."

She shrugged. "Okay."

"You're going to want to change, right? There's another bathroom, and don't forget the butler's pantry behind the bar."

Riya shook her head in amazement at the extravagance and went to go grab her regular clothes out of the suitcase that stored the microscope. As she was getting into her jeans, she heard male voices out in the room. The rest of the men must have arrived. They were coming in through different entrances, since some of them were dressed more casually.

She felt her palms sweating. Even though Gray had explained things outside the Al Dhafra Air Base, they hadn't had a chance to interact as she was getting ready to act the part of Wyatt's girlfriend.

"Ow." She hit her elbow against the sink counter when there was a knock on the door.

"Riya, are you all right?"

"Yeah, I'm fine," she told Gray.

"Can I come in?"

She opened the door. She was just putting on her shoes and socks.

How could it surprise her how tall he was? She should be used to it by now. Instead she found herself looking at an expanse of black in a tight t-shirt. She took her time wandering upwards to look at his face. Even his throat was sexy, then there was that scar on his lip and finally those blue eyes.

He pulled off the microphone around his throat and took hers off as well. He opened the bathroom door back up and threw them out. Riya heard shouts of laughter. She didn't care. Gray pulled her into his arms. He cupped the back of her head, so she was tucked safely under his chin. She could hear his heart beating.

"My Buttercup," he breathed.

"Don't you mean your Indian Buttercup?"

She'd worn her hair down, like a silken black waterfall. He tucked back a strand behind her ear.

"You're being too literal. I fell in love with Buttercup when I was seven years old and my aunts took me to see the movie. I fell in love with her because she was the one who waited for Westley, because she was his destiny. She was his one true love. Even then, I knew that was what I wanted. It had nothing to do with the color of her hair."

Her lips pursed and her eyes sparkled. "But I'm thinking you might like that she and I both have long hair."

"Careful, your genius is showing." He gripped her long hair in his fist and slammed his mouth down on hers. This was no slow seduction, it was a storm of liquid fire, and Riya grabbed for his shoulders or she would have fallen. His lips didn't soothe and tease, they forced hers open, demanding supplication, demanding a surrender she was only too happy to give.

The room whirled, and she felt her butt hit something hard. Riya realized she was sitting on the marble countertop, her legs splayed with Gray pressed hard against her core. He tasted different, like his kiss was flavored by a compulsion. She pushed at his chest.

"Gray," she panted.

He pressed his lips against her temple.

"Listen to me," she continued. "It's going to be fine. You're going to take down those bogeys or targets or tangos or assholes or whatever you want to call them. You're going to take them out, and we will go home and everything will be fine."

He lifted his head, their eyes mere inches apart.

"You believe that, don't you?" Their breath mingled.

"Absolutely. Because I believe in you. I might not know all of your team really well, but I know you're leading them, so you're going to make this work. You're going to save everybody."

"Is that what you want?" he asked with a rakish grin.

"Yes." She thumped her fist on his chest.

"As you wish."

WYATT HAD DONE good reserving the most expensive suite in the hotel. The HVAC room that controlled all of the heating and air conditioning for the entire hotel was also located on this floor.

Gray looked at his watch, then over his shoulder at Wyatt, who was staying in the room to monitor everything. "We good to go?"

"Three, two, one. Now." Wyatt gave Gray and Dex the go signal. The two of them left the hotel suite and turned left down the hallway that was no longer under surveillance. At the end of hallway was an innocuous door, and Dex took out his Smartphone. He flashed it in front of the key card pad for the door. It flashed red for three minutes, until it finally went green.

Dex grinned like a proud parent.

"What the fuck?" Gray stared at Dex in amazement.

"I calibrated it on the Palace Suite door lock. Once I had that dialed in, it was easy enough to tweak it."

"Easy my ass." Gray whispered as he opened the door. He was surrounded by bloody geniuses.

Both of them were dressed in cargo pants, black t-shirts and lightweight nylon jackets. They each carried canvass bags containing heavy weapons. Under their coats they had their Sig Sauers and knives. Their mic and receiver were the only outward indication that they might be more than they seemed, but those were fairly unobtrusive.

There had been no schematics for the interior of the HVAC room, so they were playing it by ear. As soon as they entered, Dex called out a greeting in Arabic, then again in English. They were greeted by silence. Still, they carefully swept through the room. The awards ceremony was due to start in forty-five minutes.

"Clear," Gray said.

"My side, too," Dex said as he met Gray in front of the cooling tower.

They both looked at their watches at the same time. "Get your ass moving," Dex said to Gray. "I've got it covered in here."

Gray did another quick sweep of the room and saw that there were emergency lights. He went over to the wall and turned off the lights so they were bathed in just the low red light.

"Good thinking," Dex grinned.

"That's why they pay me five dollars more a month," Gray clapped Dex on his shoulder. "Stay sharp."

He picked up his bag and left. Now it was time for a trip with Dalton.

IT WAS JUST DALTON, Aiden, Riya and Wyatt left in the room. Riya was in her blue protective suit. It made his gut clench.

"Is that really necessary?"

She still wasn't wearing the helmet, so he could see her clearly when she cocked an eyebrow.

"Gray, you suit up when you go on a mission, don't you?" she asked reasonably.

Behind her he saw Wyatt making a cutting motion along his throat. *How sad is it that Wyatt of all people is giving me advice on how to handle Riya?*

"You're right Honey, it's best that you be ready," he touched the end of her nose and gave her the best smile he could.

He looked over at Wyatt and Dalton. "Did Griff and Hunter get off okay? They're quiet."

"That's because they're not where you think they are," Wyatt said abruptly.

Gray looked at him sharply. "What are you talking about? They're supposed to be down a floor at the air handler."

"Dalton can go there," Wyatt said. "Just in case the Saudis have the wrong data too. But here's the deal. The annex building with the ballroom was built before the hotel, it's one big atrium with a two HVAC units on the roof. That's where the contagion needs to be delivered, not from where Dex is or where Dalton's going to go."

"How did we—" Gray stopped himself. This was not the time to shoulda woulda. Now was the time to come up with a new plan.

"So you've got Griff and Hunter deployed to the roof?"

"Yep."

"Gray, I have Dex's magic app on my phone. He says it'll work on the stairs, and the room with the air handler. I'm going there now," Dalton said. He stood at the door waiting for Gray's agreement.

"Go." Gray nodded.

This is not what he wanted. Griff and Hunter had dark hair and had been in suits, they were supposed to go with Aiden and mingle at the awards ceremony. Then, as if Wyatt read his mind he pointed to a neatly-folded suit on the couch. Hell, they'd even brought large leather computer bags to put the modified oxygen tanks in, so they wouldn't look *too* out of place.

"Hunter left that for you," Wyatt said.

"I'm betting it was Riya who folded it," Gray sighed. He pulled off his t-shirt and threw it on the floor as he picked up the clothes. He picked up the dress shoes and realized there wasn't a chance in hell they would fit. Hunter could be a basketball player with feet this big. He tossed them aside and figured his boots were going to have to work.

He quickly got dressed.

"Report," Gray said into his microphone.

"We're on the roof," Griff said. "Nobody's here."

"I still don't have any visitors," Dex said.

"Nobody here," Dalton said.

"Wyatt, what's the word from Midnight Delta and Night Storm?"

"Kane said that everything has been quiet at the fashion show, but that Leo has fallen in love twice since they got there."

Gray gave Wyatt a dark look.

"Okay, no more side commentary."

"Clint last reported in fifteen minutes ago. He said that Drake had seen something odd near the welcome tent at the conference. He hasn't reported in since then," Wyatt informed everyone on the communication line.

"Get ahold of Liam, I want info," Gray bit out as he tied his tie.

Maybe, just maybe, this would be a big ole nothing burger. Gray looked over at Riya who was fiddling with a microscope, and prayed with every part of his being that Dubai was the target.

"Come on Aiden, let's go."

16

THERE WERE FOURTEEN POTENTIAL TARGETS. THE KING of Jordan and his family, the Ambassador of Oman, the President of the World Bank, a Nobel Laureate, the King of Bahrain, his second wife and two sons, or one of the three journalists who had broken the story about the atrocities in Yemen. The last three weren't likely, since there were three of them, and all three had different genetic make-ups, but Langley thought that taking out any one of them might make the Saudis' point. They were all up at the dais at the front of the ballroom.

What the hell, why not just shoot one of them?

Oh yeah, they get sick, then the Saudis aren't responsible, Gray reminded himself.

Gray willed Wyatt to report something. Dex, Dalton, Griff and Hunter were still coming in with nothing, but please say that Mason had this. Any other time Gray would take on the mission and not be wishing it on another team, but another time he wouldn't have Riya in a room upstairs.

"Champagne?" a waiter asked as he walked by.

Gray shook his head. It was like he was in a James Bond movie.

Riya had explained that the gas would work best in an air conditioning vent because it would disperse the contagion throughout the space, like it had in Las Vegas. But here on the floor of the venue, it would need to be put nearer to the targets. Gray saw Aiden's blond hair moving closer to the front of the room. Thank God Abu Dhabi was such an eclectic city and blondes weren't that out of place, otherwise he and Aiden would be screwed. That was the reason Griff and Hunter were supposed to have been on this duty, they both had dark hair.

"They've got a shooter," Wyatt came in loud and clear through Gray's receiver. "Mason says they don't think he has anything to do with the potential Saudi plot, it was a lone terrorist."

Gray didn't have to ask his men if they heard, he knew they would all be on high alert.

"There!" Hunter shouted.

Aiden turned and looked at Gray, then he started meandering through the crowd as if he wasn't listening intently to his receiver.

Gray could hear a loud grunting. No gunfire, but the sound of fists on flesh was clear. Then there was the sound of metal hitting metal.

Was it the canister hitting the HVAC unit?

"Catch it!" Griff cried out.

A man yelled curse words in Arabic.

Gray started to walk quickly to the exit, when a voice came over the loudspeaker. "Is there a physician in the house?"

He turned his head and saw that the King of Jordan was leaning over his son who was slumped over the table. The King was clearly gasping for air. Gray couldn't see the wife or young daughter. Had they slipped under the table? The prince was being held up by one of the reporters.

Ah, fuck.

"We got it, Gray. We got the canister before it was deployed." Hunter said. "We're taking it to the suite."

"Aiden, find the other one," Gray said into his mic. "Find the empty one that was used on the Jordanians. Riya's going to need it."

"I'm on it."

It was rare that she had to wear her 'hot suit', but when she did, she was fanatical about it. Wyatt, God bless him, had done a second inspection for any kind of leaks before she had suited up. They had also gone through the biocontainment lab. He had helped her try to make the portable tables rest as flat as possible on the uneven floor of the bathroom.

"I don't understand why such an expensive room would have such a poorly constructed floor," Riya complained.

Wyatt laughed. "Riya, I'm pretty sure this is travertine, it's really expensive stone."

"Well it's silly. Look, the table rocks."

Wyatt had put paper under the legs to steady the table. So when Hunter had said he was coming in with a canister, she was ready for it. She put on her helmet, and air-purifying respirator, then waited.

She saw Wyatt asking her something.

She crimped the hose on her air supply, because she couldn't hear him over the hissing air. "What?"

"Riya, how well can you hear me?" Wyatt asked.

"I can now. What is it?"

"The Jordanian royal family has just been rushed to the hospital. They were the ones targeted. It makes sense that the Saudis would want them dead. Their two borders butt up to one another, and without the King or his heir, the Saudis could take over."

That had been the worst case scenario in Riya's mind. Not only did she personally like the King because he'd married a kick-ass woman with a degree in business, but Jordan had also helped America's military forces. She knew they were a target because they were currently being politically bullied by Saudi Arabia. She would do anything to help this ally of America stay alive.

"So it was the four royals?" she asked, "or were there more people in their entourage affected?"

"How did you know?" Wyatt asked.

"Because a lot of the time they have distant relatives act as assistants and bodyguards. My guess is that they might not have been as sick, unless they were a close relative."

"One lady was convulsing. A couple of others, not too bad."

Riya nodded. "Get me that canister, I'm sure I can

counteract it. If I can do this fast enough, we can get this to the hospital and save them," she said urgently. She let loose the hose so she could take a deep breath.

She thought she heard a banging, then Wyatt went and opened up the door to the suite. It was Hunter and he had his modified oxygen tank. She crimped her hose again so she could hear.

"Do you want me to put it in there?" he asked pointing to thick plastic curtains covering the bathroom entrance.

"No. What is it?" He was going too fast and she was having trouble hearing him.

"It's the tank from up on the roof. Do you want me to go put it in your clean room?" Hunter asked again.

"Does this hold the deployed canister that was used on the King and his family?" she asked as she took the modified oxygen tank out of Hunter's hands. Then she looked at his hands. She wilted. All they had were protective gloves. Just leather to keep them safe. She hated that.

The suite door opened again. It was Gray with Dex right behind him.

Gray was saying something, but she couldn't hear him. He practically yelled, so she could finally hear him in the receiver over the hiss of the air. "What are you doing?" he asked.

"Since this has the canister with the contagion used on the King, I'm going to analyze it. It should be extremely close to what I examined last month. This will just have a genetic tweak or two that I need to comprehend in order to develop the counter-sequence. Once I have that, the antivirus will take minutes to create, but it will then need to be administered as quickly as possible. It's the analyzing process that takes the longest."

"That's not the canister that was used on the Jordanians. This is the one from the roof," Gray clarified.

"Where's the one used on the King?" she asked.

"Aiden's trying to track it down."

Riya's stomach clenched. They didn't have time to waste. The amount of time it took to process things through the centrifuge, thermal cycler and then use the capillary electrophoresis and push the sequence through the fluorescence reader would take hours. Minutes mattered.

"When does Aiden think he'll be able to retrieve it?" she asked.

"They closed off the entire room. Nobody's allowed in, otherwise I'd send the whole team down to help search." Gray was obviously frustrated. "As it is, Aiden's going to have a hell of a time finding and then taking the canister out of there."

"I'm down here looking too, Gray," Dalton said in his ear.

Thank God for small miracles.

Riya took her time thinking it through. The Jordanians were the target. They would have used the same contagion in the room, and had a back-up going through the HVAC units. The triplets had all died in under sixteen hours. She needed to make a command decision.

"There's almost a hundred percent probability that

this contains the same contagion as the one in the ballroom. I need to get to work now," she decided.

Gray stepped in front of her, careful to keep space between them so he didn't touch her suit, he didn't want to risk damaging it. "Riya, are you sure?"

"Gray, be logical. What are the chances this doesn't contain the same thing?"

"Riya, it's my job to expect the unexpected. So far, things have gone wrong, so it seems to me this could, too."

"That wasn't logical," she grimaced. "What's worse, if everything had gone perfectly, you would say that *because* things had gone perfectly, now was the time that something would go wrong."

He had the good grace to look sheepish. She laughed, and it fogged the inside of her mask.

Gray looked serious, "How much time do they have to live?"

"There's a child, right?"

"A twelve-year-old girl."

"She probably has ten hours max. Using only portable equipment, it's going to take me five to six hours to get the antivirus developed, and then she'll need to be injected and have at least one to two hours for it to flow through her bloodstream. Gray, this is like meningitis. Even if she doesn't die, she can end up deaf or with brain damage."

She paused and took a deep breath.

"Gray, there just isn't any time to spare."

He nodded. "Do your thing, Buttercup."

As GRAY WATCHED her go through the inner door of the containment room, he turned on Wyatt.

"She can't hear us, right?"

"Not if we talk softly. The air hisses pretty loudly in that space suit of hers."

"Okay, then everybody speak softly." He turned to Hunter. "Where the fuck is Griffin Porter?" He was caught between concern for his team member and batshit terror for Riya.

"Griff is chasing down the guy who rappelled off the side of the roof, I was left with the canister and corpses."

"Three guys for one canister? That makes no sense," Gray said.

"Actually there were four. It was definitely overkill. Griff got his mic and receiver ripped off during the fight." Hunter fished out the broken pieces of Griff's equipment and held it up for show.

"Fuck me running," Gray groaned.

"He has his mobile, as soon as he has that fucker captured, he'll call us. He knows to take him alive."

Gray looked over his shoulder and saw Dex staring through the thick plastic. "What's going on in there?"

"She's got the oxygen tank open, and she's pulled out the canister. It's still locked shut."

Shit, they hadn't discussed how to open it.

"She's got it open now," Dex said.

Figures.

"Dex, tell me the second anything goes sideways in there, got it?"

"Roger that," Dex agreed.

Gray turned to Hunter. "Tell me what the hell

happened up on that roof. Why corpses? How did you get the canister?"

"We took the stairs to the roof. Dex's little app is handy. We were in place when I heard the Saudis climbing up the side of the wall up to the roof. There were four of them coming up the wall to begin with. When the second to the last guy came up over the wall, he cut the line on the fourth guy. The asshole killed his buddy."

Everybody stared at Hunter.

"It just gets weirder. They came up to the HVAC unit that is three meters from the edge of the roof. Griff's line of sight is blocked by that big hunk of metal, so he can't get off a shot, so he's on the run toward us. My focus is on the fucking canister in the guy's hand. It's obviously been assembled, now they just have to pop that baby in the air conditioning unit and give it a few minutes and open 'er up."

Hunter grunted as his phone rang, and he jerked open his jacket.

"She's cut open one of the gel packs, Gray," Dex said.

Gray felt sweat start to form at the base of his spine at Dex's words. He kept staring at Hunter to see if there was any word on Griff.

"Got it. Wyatt will find it. We're on our way."

"Well?" Wyatt asked from the couch as he leaned over his laptop.

"He's at Heritage Park," Hunter answered.

"Couldn't he narrow it down a bit?" Wyatt asked sarcastically.

"Yeah, he said a cricket pitch. And, because he knew

you'd ask, think a cross between a pitcher's mound and lawn bowling," Hunter threw back at him.

"Finish your story, Hunter." Gray demanded.

"Okay, but remember, Griff's Arabic is better than mine. I've got one guy down, I don't want to shoot because I don't know how fragile that damn canister is. So as I'm dispatching my guy and waiting for Griff, the two others are yelling. One is saying not to go against the King's orders. The other is saying the Prince wants them all dead. The one who's on the side of the King grabs the canister and I grab him."

"Found it. I can give you directions," Wyatt interrupted.

"Then what happened, Hunter?" Gray asked. He was beginning to understand, and it was scaring the ever loving hell out of him.

"The guy who was babbling about killing them all for the Prince grabs a rope and goes over the side of the building. Gray, he was scaring the fuck out of me. It didn't sound like the plan."

"Nope, sure didn't," Gray agreed.

"I yelled at Griff that I had the canister," Hunter said. "I told him to follow that fucker, and keep him breathing."

"Good plan," Gray agreed. Hunter gave him a long look.

"Is it as bad as I think it is?" Wyatt asked.

Hunter and Gray looked at the younger man. Each of their faces was grim.

"She's got the samples in the spinning thing. I think it's a centrifuge," Dex said.

Gray walked swiftly to stand next to Dex. He laid

his hands against the first plastic door separating him from the woman he loved. What could he tell her? What did he really know? He watched her precise movements as she wrote something down in that dog-eared notebook. His heart was breaking for that poor family.

17

Not even when she had been working on her first doctorate had something seemed to take so long as waiting for the thermal cycler to finish. She needed the results. It had been over three hours since she had loaded the sample in the thermal cycler. She flipped through the pages of her notebook, checking her formulas for any kind of flaws or oversights. She moved her microscope again. Some of the paper Wyatt had jammed under the table had come loose, and the table was rocking. Unfortunately, the paper was between the plastic covering the floor and the actual travertine floor. Not good planning.

Dammit.

Finally, she heard the ping announcing it was done. She looked at the machine. *What the heck?* The light was still red. She heard more noise.

"Riya?"

She looked over her shoulder and saw Wyatt, Aiden and Dalton. She grinned and waved. It was nice to get her mind off of the red light. She saw another one of the modified oxygen tanks in Aiden's hands and a really strange look on Wyatt's face. Scratch that, it wasn't strange.

She crimped her hose. "Wyatt, what's wrong?"

"You have to come out here to get the new tank, right?" Wyatt asked.

"Yes," she said the word slowly. "You didn't answer my question. What's wrong?"

"Riya, come out here," Aiden said in a very reassuring tone of voice.

"Sure thing. It'll take me a few minutes to decontaminate. I'll be out as quickly as I can."

Riya went through the first set of plastic doors and sprayed herself with disinfectant. She wiped the suit down. She inspected, cleaned and removed her overshoes, then disconnected the breathing line from her helmet. Not that she really needed that since she was dealing with liquids. When she went back in, she'd do without the hose, but she'd keep the helmet on, since she hadn't brought goggles or a mask. She zipped up the interior door then unzipped the outer door and took off her helmet and smiled. It was good to breathe fresh air.

"Hi, guys."

"Riya, we have a problem. We don't have confirmation yet, but Griff and Hunter are pretty sure that the canister you've been examining contains a different contagion than the one used on the Jordanian royals."

"How can you be sure?"

"Riya, we aren't one hundred percent sure. But this

all makes sense from a political standpoint. We have one of the Saudis who killed his teammate in order to silence him. Then he was going to kill another one, saying that this canister contained a poison to kill them all."

Time stopped. But it really sped up at lightning speed. How was she possibly going to condense her three lost hours into a minute? Her eyes filled with tears of frustration. That little princess was going to die.

"Give that to me," she made a grab for the metal tube that Aiden was holding.

"Wait," Wyatt said. "There's more."

"Nothing else matters," she said fiercely.

"This does. We think that the contagion you've been working on is that broad one they talked about in the briefing back in the States," Wyatt said. "That means it can kill you."

"No it can't. It's in its liquid form. Even if it wasn't, I'm following all the protocols, I'm protected."

Dalton went white, and shouldered Aiden aside. "Don't ever say something like that again, Riya. Never tempt fate."

"I—"

"Never." His eyes blazed fiercely. "Do you understand me? Promise me."

She had never seen him so shaken. This was obviously very important to him. She put her hand on his bicep.

"I promise, Dalton." Her voice was quiet and fierce.

"Good," he relaxed a little bit.

"Look, I need that canister. I have to start working on this. I'm not sure I have enough time to save them.

There's a little girl's life at stake. I promise to be careful."

Dalton took the oxygen tank from Aiden and held it while she put her helmet back on, then he handed it to her. "Remember your promise."

"I will."

"THERE." Hunter pointed to a parking spot in a secluded corner that butted up to the children's playground.

Gray and Hunter exited the Mercedes sedan at a leisurely pace, not wanting to call any attention to themselves. Most of the Abu Dhabi military and emergency personnel were at the hotel. According to Wyatt they had cordoned off the entire building where the gala had been held. Aiden and Dalton had somehow made it up to the suite. Gray would find out how they had managed that Houdini trick later, in the meantime he and Hunter needed to get information from the Saudi who had escaped.

"We see the cricket pitch," Hunter whispered into the phone. "Where are you?"

Hunter listened to Griff, then pointed to a copse of trees that were fifty meters east of the cricket field. "I see it," he said into the phone, then he put it away.

Gray was surprised to see so many people out at night. The city was very cosmopolitan. There were even a few people picnicking.

"How in the hell did Griff manage to have a chase scene in this park?" Gray asked.

"Fuck if I know," Hunter said. "Do you notice it's mostly couples and families?"

"Kind of late for families to be out."

Gray was getting sick of all the small talk as they made their way slowly across the field. But inconspicuous was the watch word.

They heard sirens, and as people turned to look, Gray took off at a jog, and Hunter followed.

Fuck taking it slow.

As soon as they made it past the tree line, they stopped and listened. Gray didn't hear anything. Looking down, the tracks were obvious. Gray took point. Another twenty meters, and they found Griff kneeling above a man who was slumped in front of him, glassy eyed, blood dripping down his face, and what looked like a sock stuffed in his mouth.

"Glad you could join the party," Griff said hoarsely. "Allow me to introduce you to Abdur Hamidi." Griff pulled at the man's hair. "Say hello, Abdur," Griff said in Arabic.

The man made a high-pitched muffled squeal, tears and blood dripping down his face. "Oh yeah, something seems to be stopping him from being all social." Gray looked closer and saw that underneath the man's strands of hair, part of his scalp had been cut up and away from his head.

Holy fuck.

"Griff, you seem a little angry," Gray kept his voice even.

"Not angry, tired. Just tired. I waited for the two of you to make sure I didn't miss anything. We've got a big one on our hands."

How come he wasn't surprised?

"Our friend here explained to me that his brother is a scientist, who came up with a poison that was supposed to take out specific families. He did this for his King. You know the old guy, rules Saudi Arabia?" Griff gave a half smile.

"Shit," Hunter said. "It goes all the way to the top."

"Yep. So the King decided to try out his new toy to make sure it was in working order, before the big show, which was tonight's grand finale. Apparently, he wants to take over a neighboring country. Simple enough, right?" Griff shook his head in disgust.

"Let me guess," Gray broke in. "The King's power hungry son had a different idea."

"Hunter, give this man a cigar. I like our boss, he's smart. He should date a genius."

Hunter gave a short laugh, and Gray scowled at him.

"So, that's what I heard on the roof? This asshole was going to send down a contagion that was going to kill everyone?" Hunter asked.

"Yep."

"We need to find his brother," Gray said.

"That was my take," Griff agreed. "He's given me a location. It's here in the city, but I don't trust him. What's more, it's not like I can drag his ass out through the flower children in the park. They freaked out as we ran through. I think they thought we were playing some sort of game the first time. Him all bloody isn't going to cut it now. Pun intended."

Gray crouched down in front of the man and

grabbed his hair. "Where is your brother?" he asked in Arabic.

The man's eyes got wide and his shriek could be heard even with the sock in his mouth. "I won't kill you. However, I will cut off your scalp, then I will scrape the skin off your cock, if you don't tell me the truth. Do you understand?" Gray continued in Arabic.

Hunter pulled out his knife and twirled it in front of the man's face.

Gray watched as a large snot bubble formed and popped.

He took the knife from Hunter and placed it at the tip of the sniveling man's nose, and pulled the sock out of his mouth.

"Talk."

Thank God she didn't have the hose hissing air at her anymore, she could hear herself think. Riya looked at the green light on the thermal cycler. She pulled out the samples that were useless, at least for now. She also pulled the slides out of the microscope. The one thing she didn't have was an autoclave, which shouldn't have been a problem, because she was supposed to have been working with only one contagion. Riya got out the disinfectant spray and cleaned everything she could, as thoroughly as she could.

Calm.

Breathe.

Think.

Calm.

Breathe.

Think.

Riya tried to imagine herself in her own lab. She had a microscope. It wasn't her microscope, but it was a microscope. She looked over the table at all the other equipment. It was familiar, maybe not hers, but still familiar. Then she felt her heartbeat slow when she saw her black and white notebook. She could do this.

Her hands were now steady.

The table wobbled. Great. Her hands were steady, but the table wasn't.

Just freaking great.

Riya made sure everything associated with the broad contagion was put over to the right side of the table. She would work on the Jordanian contagion on the left side of the table.

She took the modified oxygen tank and opened it. She pulled out the deployed canister. The top part was missing. Carefully, she pulled out the bottom part and placed it on her table. She would need a substantial sample to pull off a miracle. Granted, when she'd been in D.C. she'd worked with a miniscule amount, but she'd had the best equipment in the world. Now, she needed a lot of the contagion.

The liquid was too thick to pour out of the canister, so she was going to need to reach inside to the bottom with an eyedropper. She gently tapped the metal on the table, trying to make it all fall to one side. She said a little prayer, and went for it. *Please let there be enough to get a good sample.*

"Ow!"

She dropped the eyedropper. Something sharp inside the canister had scraped her. Was it some kind of boobie-trap? She bit her lip. She fished around for the eyedropper and worked to extract her sample. She grinned when she pulled out a full load. It would be more than enough.

Riya looked at her torn glove and the small scrape on her hand.

Fuck!

She froze. Then blew out a deep breath as she realized this was the DNA specific contagion, thank the Lord. She was good, but long years of protocol demanded she get a new pair. She reached over to the glove box. The table wobbled and the canister rolled and hit her elbow. She stumbled two steps to the right, her scraped hand landing on a slide with the broad contagion.

She jerked her hand back and cradled it to her chest.

For the second time that day, time stopped.

Her mind blanked.

How long did she stand like that? Frozen? Unable to move?

Calm.

Breathe.

Think.

How was she supposed to think? How?

"Riya?

"Riya?

"Are you all right?"

It was Wyatt's voice.

She let go of her hand and forced both of them

down to her sides. She turned, thankful her face was obscured by the helmet.

"I'm fine, Wyatt." If she asked a question, he wouldn't question her. "Where's Gray? When is he coming back?"

"Griff needed a lift back to the hotel. He should be back in an hour."

"Okay. Got to get back to it."

"How is it going?" Wyatt asked.

"Got a sample to work with from the new canister. I'll be able to create an antivirus in under four hours. Do you have any idea how the Jordan royal family is doing?"

Wyatt rubbed the top of his thigh. It was the first time she saw him do something to indicate his injury still bothered him. "I haven't been able to. Dex is trying to work his magic now." He seemed sad. Riya finally understood that he was upset that Dex was better than he was.

"Shouldn't you be over there learning what he's doing?"

"I guess so."

"You'll never get any better at this if you don't learn."

"I want to be on the team. Out in the field with Hunter. Not stuck in here working communications."

Her hand throbbed. She needed to get started. "You mean Dex is somehow less than the others on the team because he does communications?"

Wyatt was quiet for a long moment. Finally he shook his head. "I'm a dumbshit."

"So it would seem. I have to get to work."

Wyatt walked away and she turned around. Her neck was beginning to ache just a little. That was the first sign of meningitis. She had been inoculated for the disease back in D.C. when she realized what she was working with. It seemed to be helping keep the symptoms at bay. Maybe she had time to get the antivirus created before the Princess died.

Wait a minute. What the hell was she thinking? She could do two things at once. She couldn't believe she was such a defeatist. Riya grabbed the broad contagion that had gone through the thermal cycler. She quickly prepped it and put it into the fluorescence reader.

Finally she could breathe again. She would have both antiviruses made up.

One for her, and one for the royals.

A sense of peace flowed through her.

18

"GUYS, IT'S NOT A VALID ADDRESS," DEX SAID OVER THEIR receiver. Hunter relayed the news to Griff.

Gray relayed the news in Arabic to the man, who babbled back in Arabic.

"I heard him," Dex said. "I'm checking it out." Gray could hear the familiar sound of Dex slamming down on the keyboard. "Got it, he's outside of the forty-fourth sector, on the north side of third street."

"Dalton. Aiden. Do you think you can get past all the patrols, find a vehicle and meet us at the address?" Gray asked.

"Not a problem." Aiden's voice was confident.

Gray didn't want anything to go wrong. This guy needed to be caught. God knew how many different formulas he'd made.

"Riya, can you hear me?" Gray asked.

"Loud and clear," she answered. Her voice was subdued.

"You all right?"

"Just saying plenty of prayers I can have the antivirus done in time for the little girl."

"What's your ETA?" Gray asked.

"Just got everything started forty-five minutes ago."

She sounded off, but maybe this was just how Riya sounded in scientist mode.

"Gray, Dalton and Aiden have already left," Dex said.

"Good. That's good," he muttered.

"Yeah, well, here's the not-so-good part," Dex said. "Liam has been up my ass ever since you've been gone. Then Captain Hale started in an hour ago, and I just got pinged a half hour ago by the lieutenant general who has to brief the president."

"Why, the president?"

"The president is going to be the one who has to smooth the way with the Emirate of Abu Dhabi to get the antivirus into the Jordanian royals, then there is the prime minister of Jordan. The president's got to start cutting through the red tape like yesterday."

Gray hadn't considered that. He turned to Hunter. "Let's go. You're going to need to drop me off at the hotel so I can deal with the brass, while you head over to the address."

RIYA STARTED TO SHIVER. Even in her hot suit, she was cold. She so badly wanted to rub the back of her neck. Her head was pounding. These were all the signs of meningitis. While she waited for the thermal cycler to finish for the DNA specific contagion, she had the fluorescence reader working on the broad contagion.

She heard a commotion and turned around.

"Gray." Her head was swimming.

She carefully walked a straight line to the plastic inner door and gave a wan smile.

"Hey, Buttercup."

She looked behind him.

"Wyatt said you would be gone for an hour. It's been a lot longer than that. Where's everybody else?"

Gray grimaced. "It takes a while to get in and out of the hotel. Cops and the military are swarming around. The others are on an assignment. I'm here to talk to some people. How's it going for you? I know you had to start over."

He looked sad.

"I don't know if I'm going to get the antivirus developed in time to save the girl." Riya was beginning to feel nauseous.

Please don't let me be sick inside my helmet.

"Gray, I have to get back to work."

"Understood. So do I," he grimaced.

She gave a brief nod, and instantly regretted it. Her head hurt. She turned and walked gingerly back to the table. As she got closer, she saw the green light was on the thermal cycler. Her eyes darted to the fluorescence reader, the timer still said thirty-five minutes. She wanted to cry.

Riya pulled out the samples from the two machines, and put the DNA-specific ones into the fluorescence reader. The Jordanian family needed to live. It was the right decision to make. Maybe if she taught someone what to do after she got too sick to keep going, they could work on the broad contagion?

What happened if they got infected like she did?

"GRAY?" Wyatt waved his hands so he couldn't be seen on the SKYPE call. He knew it must be important since he was now on a call with the lieutenant general and an admiral.

"Please give me a few minutes to confer with Dr. Patel, and I'll find out the ETA on the antivirus."

Both men nodded. Gray turned off the microphone on the computer, and got off the couch. He saw that Dex was now standing beside the outer door of the biocontainment lab. "Does Riya know how much longer? It's been six hours and ten minutes." Gray strode over to stand by Dex. "Riya said five to six hours."

It was unlike her to be wrong on something like this. He'd expected her to be closer to five hours.

He looked through the curtain. Riya was leaning on the lab table. Her hand trembled as she poured something into a beaker.

"She hasn't answered for five minutes, Gray," Dex said. "She went to her knees once, but got back up. She hasn't stopped working. The last thing she said is that she almost has the antivirus for the Princess."

"Riya?" Gray called out.

She didn't respond in any way.

"Riya, answer me." Gray's tone was sharp.

"Hold on."

He could barely hear her, her voice was hoarse. Something was wrong.

"She's been standing up for hours. That suit is known as a hot-suit. I googled it, they are miserable to work in. I think she's probably suffering from heatstroke," Wyatt said, trying to calm Gray down.

"Riya, Honey. Talk to me."

"I can make it. I'm going to make it."

Those ominous words sent shivers down his spine.

"Are you sick?" He asked in a choked voice.

She turned and stumbled down to one knee, but the beaker stayed clutched in her hand. Gray held his breath as she got up and continued to walk unsteadily toward the door.

"Riya, answer me, are you sick? Did you get some of the contagion on you?" She ignored him, and continued to walk. With one trembling hand she managed to unzip the interior door, zip it back up and go through the disinfectant routine.

She took off her helmet in the area, and looked directly at Gray, her eyes glassy, her face red with fever.

"I put on two pairs of new gloves over my hands after I ripped the first pair. I swear you won't be contaminated with the broad contagion. What's more, this strain of meningitis is not communicable, I promise."

Gray thought his knees might give out.

"Steady," Dex said.

He and Dex both dove for the bottom of the outer door zipper. They got it unzipped. Dex got the beaker out of Riya's hands and she fell into Gray's arms. He could feel the heat emanating off her.

"How much?" Dex demanded.

What the fuck was he talking about?

Gray was pulling at the suit, trying to get it off her.

"So cold. I'm so cold." Her teeth were chattering. Her hair was drenched in sweat, her face was beet red.

"Riya, how much do we need to administer?" Dex articulated clearly.

She looked at him glassy eyed. "Same dosage amount as meningococcal vaccine," she said softly. Then she started to cough.

They heard the distinctive sound of the SKYPE call coming in. "Dex, answer it," Gray snarled. "Give them the update." He turned to Wyatt. "Get me every goddamn blanket in this goddamn room."

Gray sank to the floor and started rocking Riya in his arms.

"Don't move," she begged in a tortured whisper. "Going to vomit."

"Riya, Honey, do you have the antivirus for your poison? Is it in the lab?"

"Only antivirus for royal family. No time for me."

Gray shuddered with agony. Wyatt came and started swaddling her in blankets. "I've called for an ambulance. Dex told the brass. They're notifying the president."

"Get the antivirus to the family. Please Gray. Save them." He could barely hear her. Her eyes were filled with hope, right before her eyelids drifted shut.

"As you wish."

She didn't answer.

"Riya! Wake-up!" He shook her. She convulsed.

IT WAS AMAZING what could happen when the King of the Universe cut all the red tape. Members of their special operations came with a doctor to pick up the beaker with the antitoxin, and a mere minute later the EMT's for Riya arrived. Gray wouldn't have been surprised if they loaded Riya onto a stretcher made of gold. There were at least fifteen soldiers escorting her to the lobby.

"Gray," a familiar voice yelled as he was hovering over Riya's stretcher. He looked up and saw Mason coming in from one of the doors. He ran over, one of the CDC scientists in his wake. Mason glanced down at Riya and blanched.

"I've got Jeff here," he said pointing to the scientist. "Wyatt has been keeping us informed. We're here to help find the antivirus for Riya."

Gray nodded grimly. He couldn't take the time to talk. "Wyatt. Keep talking to Wyatt," he said as he went out the door with the EMT's.

When the ambulance tech inserted an IV into Riya's arm, he saw purplish spots forming on her arm. Gray had read up on meningitis. This was bad, it was one of the later symptoms of the disease.

The ambulance ride was long, his eyes never left Riya's face.

Gray tried to pick up his men on his receiver. It wasn't working. Too many machines in the ambulance.

He pulled out his cell phone. "Sir, you can't use your cell phone in the ambulance," the tech said.

"This is an emergency." Gray said in his officer voice.

"You will interfere with the machines that are helping to keep this woman alive, do you want to do that?"

Gray put his cell phone back in his pocket.

He trusted his men to do what was right.

He knelt down beside the gurney where Riya rested. He picked up her hand and brought it to his lips. "Stay with me, Riya. I can't live in this world without you." He watched as tears washed over the soft skin of her hand.

THE RECEIVER WAS TWISTED plastic in his hand. It had been worthless before he had crushed it. He tried to make sense of what Dalton was saying to him on his cell phone.

"He must have taken some of his own stuff, his body was bloated beyond recognition. Griff brought over the guy's brother. He and Aiden are trying to make sense of all the beakers and vials that are stored in the five different refrigerators, and strewn across his lab. Gray, it's a pigsty. Everything's written in Arabic, and none of us read it. We're dependent on Hamidi." Dalton's anguish and frustration came through the phone in waves.

"What about the UAE people, now that we're not running dark?"

"Dex and Wyatt are already on it. They're expected to arrive any minute."

Gray stared at the small figure that Riya made as

she lay in the hospital bed. Her presence was normally so big, and now she seemed so diminished.

"Gray?"

"Yeah?" He could barely get the word out.

"There's still time, right?" Dalton asked.

"They say with all of her symptoms, even if the antivirus is administered she could come out of this deaf or brain damaged."

There was a long silence. After all, what could Dalton say. Finally his friend said, "I'll pray for her."

"Thank you." Gray hung up the phone.

Time had no meaning. He remembered the first time he saw her. Those flashing dark eyes. Her sweetness wrapped in vulnerability. He had never met anyone like her. That's because there wasn't anyone like Riya Patel.

The morning he went to shave in the bathroom and found that heart she'd drawn on the mirror. Suddenly he wondered who was taking care of Einstein.

"Who cares about the damn cat!"

Those white high heels.

"Please come back to me Riya. Please."

"Let us through!"

Gray's head popped up from where it was resting on her hand. It was Wyatt's voice and he was angry. Gray, jumped up from the floor, his knee locking up.

More shouting, this time in Arabic. He heard the soothing sound of Mason Gault's voice. The doctor who was in charge of Riya walked in with the CDC guy and Mason, Wyatt trailing behind.

"Where's Dalton?"

"Jeff found what Riya had been working on. She'd been halfway through with completing the antivirus for the broad contagion," Mason said.

Gray wasn't getting it, and it must have shown. The doctor had a syringe and he opened up the port on Riya's IV.

"Stop!" Grabbed his arm. "What are you doing?" He turned to Mason and Wyatt.

"Explain this to me."

"Gray," Wyatt said. "Trust us. It's going to make her well. You've got to believe us. She needs it now."

Mason put his hand on his shoulder. "Jeff did it. Riya had it halfway done and Jeff just finished it. Let the doctor administer the drug."

Gray let go of the doctor, who then plunged the syringe into the port.

"Riya said it would take one to two hours to work, is that right? Will she wake up then?"

"I really don't know," the doctor shook his head.

"What happened to the royal family? Are they awake? What about the little girl? They got the drug hours ago."

"The King and his son are awake and alert. The queen is sleeping, but she did wake up at one point. We're still waiting to see what happens to with the princess. The good news is that she's responding to stimuli and scoring well on the Glasgow scale, so we have high hopes."

"So how soon will we know if this is working for Riya?" Gray persisted.

"We are administering her antivirus exactly ninety minutes later than we did the one for the royal family, so I don't know. The good news is that according to her records, she had the meningococcal vaccine, that's to her favor." The doctor must have seen the desperation in his face. "I heard how long she lasted after being infected. What she accomplished was a miracle. She's going to pull through."

Gray turned his head to his friends and saw Mason and Wyatt nodding their heads in agreement.

RIYA NEVER REMEMBERED HURTING this bad. She couldn't move her neck. Her eyes wouldn't open. Why wouldn't her eyes open?

"My name is Inigo..." she couldn't hear the rest. She was so tired. The voice sounded so familiar. Was it her father?

No, that wasn't right. But it was such a warm and comforting voice. She felt safe.

SHE FELT sunlight on her face. She heard that voice again. This time it was hoarse, but...

It was Gray and he was talking about the Dread Pirate Roberts from the Princess Bride. She still couldn't move her neck. But this time she could lift her eyelids. She wet her lips.

"Gray?"

Was that her voice?

"Riya?"

She was tired again. Her eyes drifted shut.

———

"...AND that's why I liked this movie, and the book is pretty good too, now that I've read it to you. Shall I start again?"

"It was the love story, wasn't it?" she croaked out. "You're gooey."

Hands crashed down on either side of her pillow. Sky blue eyes blazed down at her. "Don't you dare close your eyes again."

"I'm here?"

"What's two plus two?" Gray asked.

"Four."

"What country are the great pyramids in?"

"Egypt?"

"What's Pi?"

"3.14159-"

"Enough!"

He slammed his lips down on hers.

Eeeewww. She needed a toothbrush. She tried to turn her head, but her neck hurt too badly.

"Kiss me back," Gray murmured.

"No. Wanna toothbrush."

"I love you." Slowly he brushed his nose against hers.

EPILOGUE

She wasn't going to be put off another second. She would fly to Washington D.C. if she had to. It had been three flipping weeks since she had been home, and she still didn't have an answer. She squirmed into her dress, and tried to reach her zipper, but it was too far in the back.

"Dammit!"

Einstein yowled and jumped off the bed, then stalked out of the room.

"Need some help?" Gray asked as he sidestepped her cat and wandered into the bedroom.

"I so shouldn't have bought this dress. It's Susan's fault," Riya huffed.

Gray put gentle hands on her shoulders and looked at the yellow sheath dress that lovingly accentuated every one of her curves. "I'm going to have to thank Susan the next time I see her," Gray said as he zipped up her dress.

Riya bit her lip. "Isn't this a little over the top?

Where are we having dinner?"

"You'll know when we get there," Gray smiled.

"I hate surprises."

"I know. Now tell me what has you so worked up. Besides the zipper."

She went to the closet and pulled out the white pair of heels she'd worn to the wedding. She saw Gray's appreciative smile and heat coiled inside. Dinner out was nice, but coming home was going to be even nicer.

"Let me help with those," Gray said as she sat down on the bed.

She held out a foot and Gray took his time putting on her right shoe. "Riya, tell me what has you so fired up."

"I want to know what kind of retribution is going to happen to the Saudis. They can't get away with that. It's wrong on so many levels. General Astor has to know something, but he isn't coming clean."

"He's not going to tell you," Gray said as he put on her left shoe.

"But he has to. If not me, then you. You're in the military, don't they tell you things? Don't they tell you what happens to the bad guys?"

Gray burst out laughing. "You have got to be kidding. We just do our little job and stay in our bubble. We're never informed about anything after the mission is done."

Gray winked at her.

What did that mean?

"Why did you wink?"

He smiled, and continued to kneel at her feet.

"That means that what you said isn't true. Right?

Did I figure it out?" She thought she was right. She was beginning to know when he was teasing.

"Yes, Sweetheart. Part of it is true, they never tell us, but...we find out things on our own. Dex is very, very good at finding out information. It seems that the King of Jordan is taking some steps at retribution. Right now it is in its early stages, but it's going to be substantial."

"What is it?" Riya was bouncing on the bed.

"It could go a few different ways. But in a few months you'll be seeing it on the evening news. The King is so good, it won't even look like it was done by his country, but you can be damn sure it was handled by him. And the Prince will know too. You don't mess with the King of Jordan's family and get away with it."

"Thank God," Riya said fervently.

"Now can we go to dinner?" Gray asked.

She threw her hands around his neck. "Absolutely."

GRAY'S HEART WAS OVERFLOWING. Riya cinched it with the bloodthirsty episode in the bedroom. She fit him in every single way imaginable. Not that this would have mattered. He was going to seize her no matter what.

He parked his SUV at the restaurant. He saw all of his friends' vehicles in the parking lot as well, and it cracked him up that Riya didn't pick up on it. But that wasn't her skill set. She was on another plane of existence, that's what made them the perfect couple.

Gray fingered the little velvet box in his suit pocket.

"Gray, this is a fancy restaurant."

"Yes, it is. That's why we're dressed fancy."

He escorted her in, and the hostess whisked them to a door at the back of the restaurant. "Are you ready?"

"What do you mean?" she asked.

Gray opened the door.

A cacophony of voices yelled 'Surprise'.

***

RIYA SHOOK. Gray put his arm around her. He seemed to always know what she needed. He pressed his mouth close to her ear. "It's all friends, Honey. All friends."

She relaxed, just a little. Then she slowly looked around the large table from face to face to face. Gray was right. Every single person was a friend.

Miranda stood and held up a glass. "To a genuine hero. Hurrah."

Each member of Black Dawn then slowly stood up, their faces solemn. "To our hero."

"You fucking rocked it," Wyatt called out.

She reached out to her right and gripped Gray's arm with everything she had.

"You're seated at the head of the table," Susan gestured. "We ordered family style."

"Good, because this is too overwhelming to figure out what I want to eat."

Gray held out the chair for her.

Before she could blink, there was a peach Bellini placed in front of her. Susan winked. Riya laughed. She took a healthy swig.

"Watch it, Lady," Gray said. "I know tonight's overwhelming, but I do want you capable of making some decisions."

"I want something chocolate for dessert," Riya said decisively.

"Well, that's good." His grin was wicked.

He pushed out his chair and turned hers so they were knee to knee. "But I'm hoping I have something better than chocolate to offer you."

Riya's gut clenched. This was serious. She looked into his eyes, they shined like diamonds. It was *really* serious. But she saw it was all about love. Whatever it was, it was good.

She knew that this was a man she could always believe in, that she could trust her life and her future to, because he would always love her.

He pulled out a velvet box, and before he had a chance to open it, before he had a chance to say a word, she sighed her answer. "Yes, Gray. Always and forever. Yes."

Riya thought she heard something like a roar in the background, but she wasn't sure. It was possible that people were clapping but it was as if she were surrounded by Gray's love. She held out her hand and he smiled. He opened the box, and slipped on her ring.

"As you wish," he said.

———

THANK you for reading *Her Captivated Hero*. For more Military Romance check out my Midnight Delta series. *Her Vigilant SEAL*, Book 1 is free.

Get your copy of Her Vigilant SEAL here.

ABOUT THE AUTHOR

USA Today Bestselling Author, Caitlyn O'Leary, adores writing Military Romantic Suspense and Paranormal Romance. She started publishing books in 2014. Storytelling has been a tradition in her family for years, and she still holds on to the letters she has received from family members since her childhood.

Caitlyn lives in California with her husband John of sixteen years who often makes guest appearances in her reader group, Caitlyn's Crew. Getting to know so many people within the reader community is almost as much fun as writing each new novel. So join her reader group so she can get to know you, and see if she and John can make it to year seventeen!

You never know what kind of book she'll write next, it all depends on what strikes her fancy. Be sure to keep in touch.

Keep up with Caitlyn O'Leary:

Website: www.caitlynoleary.com
Email: caitlyn@caitlynoleary.com
Newsletter: http://bit.ly/1WIhRup

ALSO BY CAITLYN O'LEARY

Printed in Great Britain
by Amazon